PILGRIM

Lifepath Adventures: Pilgrim Fathers

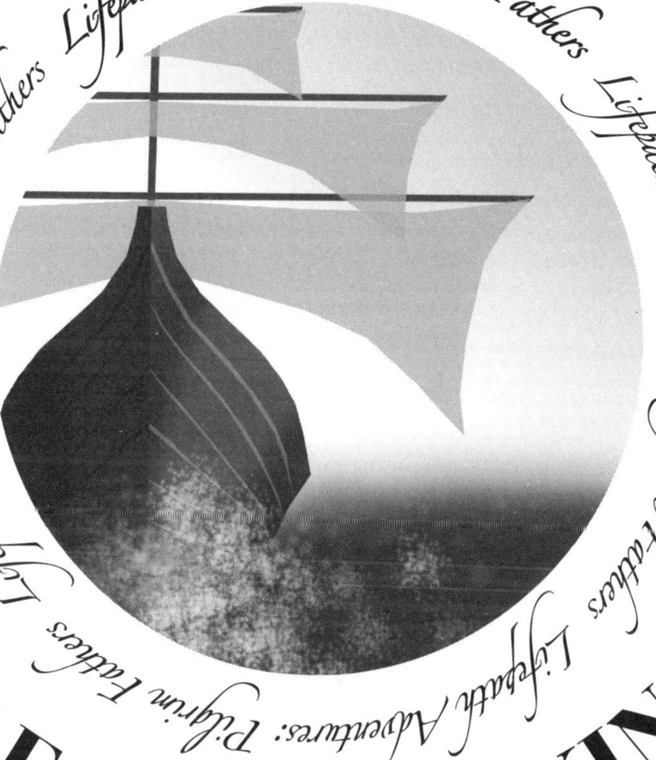

ELEANOR WATKINS

© Eleanor Watkins 2009
First published 2009
ISBN 978 1 84427 373 7

Scripture Union,
207–209 Queensway, Bletchley, Milton Keynes, MK2 2EB
Email: info@scriptureunion.org.uk
Website: www.scriptureunion.org.uk

Scripture Union Australia
Locked Bag 2, Central Coast Business Centre, NSW 2252
Website: www.scriptureunion.org.au

Scripture Union USA
PO Box 987, Valley Forge, PA 19482
Website: www.scriptureunion.org

All rights reserved. No part of this publication may be reproduced, stored in a retrieval system, or transmitted in any form or by any means, electronic, mechanical, photocopying, recording or otherwise, without the prior permission of Scripture Union.

The right of Eleanor Watkins to be identified as author of this work has been asserted by her in accordance with the Copyright, Designs and Patents Act 1988.

Scripture quotations are taken from the King James Bible.

British Library Cataloguing-in-Publication Data.
A catalogue record of this book is available from the British Library.

Printed and bound in India by Thomson Press India Ltd

Cover design: Pink Habano
Internal layout: Author and Publisher Services

Scripture Union is an international Christian charity working with churches in more than 130 countries, providing resources to bring the good news about Jesus Christ to children, young people and families and to encourage them to develop spiritually through the Bible and prayer.

As well as our network of volunteers, staff and associates who run holidays, church-based events and school Christian groups, we produce a wide range of publications and support those who use our resources through training programmes.

*For
Aidan and Dylan, whose mother
first showed me the Plimouth Plantation*

Chapter One

Alone

Not a breath of air stirred the heavy, stifling heat of the late summer afternoon. The leaves of the big oak sheltering the churchyard wall were dusty and motionless, and away over the housetops a distant rumble of thunder promised a storm on the way. Tom felt sweat trickle down the back of his neck under his shirt as he listened to the thud of earth clods on wood, watching as the gravedigger flung spadefuls of soil onto the plain coffin.

Old Mother Entwistle plucked at his sleeve. "All over now, lad. Come thee with me, have a sup of ale to slake thy thirst."

Already the black-clad minister, who had been called in to conduct what was to him just another pauper's funeral, was moving away, together with the undertaker's men, also in black. They took no notice of Tom, maybe thinking him to be in the care of a grandmother. But Mother Entwistle was just a neighbour; she and Tom's mother had known each other a little, living in the same row of small poor houses in Bear Lane. She was aged and bent, stiff with rheumatic pain and hardly able to stand straight, not far from death herself, or so it seemed to Tom. She had hobbled to the burial out of pity for the skinny boy left alone to face an uncertain future. Maybe she hoped, now his mother was gone, that he might be a source of comfort and help to her in the time remaining to her. She tugged again at his sleeve.

"Come thee away, lad. Nowt here for thee now."

Tom pulled away. Mother Entwistle had been good to his mother, as far as she was able, grateful for the kindness shown to her by the younger woman in her own times of need. But he shuddered at the thought of going back to that miserable dwelling, with rats scuttling at night and leaks dripping when it rained. Most of all, it held the memories of his mother, growing thinner and weaker by the day as her cough worsened. She had tried to do her work and stay strong for him, but day by day lost a little more of her frail grip on life.

The old woman gave him a long look out of watery blue eyes, heaved a sigh and turned to hobble away. He was really no concern of hers, after all. Best leave him to himself if that was the way his mind was set. Happen some kin of his would show themselves, though there'd been little sign of anyone when they'd been needed...

Muttering to herself, she shuffled away and out of the small gate at the end of the neglected patch of the churchyard reserved for the burials of paupers.

Left alone, Tom rubbed his knuckles into his eyes and wiped his nose on his shirt sleeve. The grave was filling fast, the sweating gravedigger anxious to finish the job and get home for a bite and a sup before the storm came. Another rumble of thunder sounded beyond the heavy, yellowish sky.

Tom turned away. It was true, there was nothing for him here. Nothing anywhere. No point in going back to the house in Bear Lane. No point in anything.

But he was hungry. His stomach told him so, rumbling and complaining, reminding him he'd eaten nothing since he'd finished the last of the cold pease pudding made by his mother on the day before she died. To the very last, she'd thought of him, dragging her body from the bed and stirring the fire into life with the sticks he'd brought in, dropping oatmeal into the pot with trembling fingers. She'd been unable to eat herself, sinking exhausted back onto the rumpled bedding. And by the next day she had gone.

A rich, meaty smell came from the open door of a house in Church Street as he left the graveyard. He paused, sniffing. Venison pasty, maybe, or mutton stew with dumplings! The kind of things they'd had for dinner, once, when times were good. He licked his lips. A young woman came out of the doorway, pausing for a moment to get a breath of air and relief from her stuffy kitchen. Beside her a baby in a white cap toddled on leading strings. The woman saw Tom loitering and picked up the baby, holding it protectively closer to her. Then she looked again.

"Art tha hungry, lad?"

Tom could only nod, his stomach rumbling again and his tongue coming out to moisten his lips. The young woman turned and went inside, returning with a hunk of bread and a lump of stale-looking cheese. "There, take that and be off home with thee."

The food put new life into Tom. He ate it, stuffing it ravenously into his mouth, sitting against a tumbledown wall in some waste ground at the back of the church, among tall nettles and docks and long dusty grass, with a hungry robin hopping around in search of stray crumbs. Overhead, the thunder grew fainter and rumbled away to the east, the sky slowly clearing. The storm had passed them by after all.

Beyond the church, the hum of the town sounded faintly: wheels on cobbles, hoofbeats, voices, clanging and clattering noises as people went about their business. Tom thought of the good days, when his father was still there and they lived comfortably on his cooper's wages, and there was food on the table, and laughter, and good clothes and stout boots to keep out the winter's chill. There had been other children, too. He frowned in concentration, remembering. Sisters – Sarah and Ellen, fair-haired and merry, younger than him, but growing fast and getting to be good company, even for girls. Then the sickness, with chills and sweating, which carried them off within days, and Mam's weeping and Father silent, and then absent more and more. There had been more babies – a boy, John, who died after being bitten by a dog when he had just begun to toddle, and then another, who lived only a few days. Try as he might, Tom could not remember whether that last baby had been a boy or a girl, or if it had a name.

It was after that last baby that things changed again, rapidly and for the worse. Mam had been sad and silent, Father angry. Then Father was gone.

"It was the drink, in the end," was all that his mother could tell him about his father's going. He gathered, from bits of gossip here and there, that his father had been dismissed from his work, and then one day just never came home.

Yet his mother would not speak badly of her husband, even when they were forced to leave their comfortable home and move to the mean house in Bear Lane.

"He was always one for new adventures," she said wistfully, frowning over the sewing that she took in, along with washing and mending, to make their meagre living. "Used to talk about going off to sea, making his fortune, coming back and buying me silks and laces..."

She sighed, and put in more small stitches. Tom could see that she half-believed his father would yet come and make things right. For himself, he hated his father with a strong loathing, for bringing them to hardship and breaking his mother's heart. And when his mother sickened and grew weak, his hatred grew.

He spoke of this one day, when his mother's coughing was so bad that she could not hold the needle. "If I ever saw him again, I would punch his teeth right down his throat," he said fiercely, clenching his hands into fists. She laid a hand on his arm, and he could feel its trembling. "No, no, Tom, never say that. However we're wronged, we must forgive. It's God's command to us. Forgive, as he forgives us sinners for the sake of his Son..." But her words ended in a fit of fresh coughing.

Sitting in the tall grass by the stone wall, Tom felt his fists clench again. "I hope he's dead too," he muttered, and the tears of grief and anger prickled his eyes again. "And if he's not, I hope he's hungry, and lonely, and – and – I hope I never see him again, for I'll never, never, forgive him."

He cried for a little, while the robin hopped curiously around him in the trodden grass, and the sun came out from behind the storm clouds. He wondered what he should do, where he should go, and suddenly, into his mind came other words of his mother's.

"Tom, if ever I— if ever you're left alone, go to Scrooby."

"Scrooby?"

He knew the town they lived in was called Gainsborough, but he'd never heard of Scrooby.

"Yes. Scrooby is the little town I came from. A small place, but busy and prosperous. Friendly folk. Country people, and farming land all about. A big church amidst the houses. My folks are dead now, but there are good people there. They would help, if need be."

"You mean the people at the church?"

She'd shaken her head. "No – though the people there are good too, I have no doubt. No, there are people called the Separatists, who believe that God will and can have dealings with one and all, high or low, without the aid of priest or empty ritual, and that all may pray and preach God's word freely as they will."

She'd coughed a little, and gone on, "When I lived there, some had been driven out, across the sea, to find their liberty. But maybe some remain, or their kin. There were some in this town too, but them I never knew – your father was against religion of any kind. But these are good people, kind, merciful. They would give aid, if... if you should have need of it. It is reached going to the west, until you come to the Great Road."

Tom had listened with half an ear. He was uneasy when his mother talked like this. But now her words came back clearly, and he understood what she had meant. She had known she could not live long. She wanted him to go there. Scrooby. There was nothing for him here, nothing anywhere, now that she was gone.

To Scrooby he must go.

Chapter Two

The Great Road

Tom's mother had told him that the Great Road would not be difficult to find, that it lay westward across the fields, and that many people travelled that road. Next morning, at first light, he set off, with the rising sun behind him, with no money, no possessions and only the much-mended and threadbare shirt, breeches, stockings and shoes that he stood up in. He had not gone back to Bear Lane, but spent the night on the straw of an outhouse at one of the dwellings on the edge of the town.

To his surprise, as dawn began to break, a brown hen, which had somehow avoided being shut up for the night, sauntered in, settled for a while in a corner and then strolled out again, leaving a large brown egg on the straw. Investigation showed that a further six or seven eggs were there too, half-covered in straw. In spite of himself, Tom grinned – he remembered times when one of their own hens would decide to 'steal' a nest – hiding her eggs where no one could collect them, and then brooding them until a family of chicks was hatched and proudly brought out into the open.

He silently thanked the brown hen, broke the morning's egg and the two freshest-looking of the others, and swallowed them down raw from their shells. A fresh spring bubbled nearby; after the food, drink and rest, he felt hope and new life spring up inside him.

Though barely light, farmers on the land surrounding the town were already going about their work. Cattle were being driven home for morning milking; as soon as the early dew lifted, harvesters would be setting out for the fields of barley and rye standing ripe and ready to be gathered. Stubble fields, already harvested, gleamed gold in the first rays of sunshine. It was going to be a fine sunny day.

Tom kept to the shelter of the hedgerows, glad of their thickly-leaved cover. By noon he had reached the road, a wide straight highway left by the Romans centuries ago, or so he had been told. Other travellers were going up and down, on foot or horseback or in trundling farm carts, intent on their business. No one took much notice of a lone 11-year-old boy making his way south.

By the time the sun was high overhead, the breakfast of eggs seemed to Tom like a distant memory, and he was hungry and thirsty again. The sun beat down mercilessly, dust rose from the road, kicked up by hooves and wheels, his much-darned stockings had rubbed through at the heels and blisters were forming.

He rested for a while, looked for water without success, got up and walked again. There was less traffic on the road now, after the morning rush. Around him in the fields harvesting went on, scythes flashed in the sun, women and children chattered as they set the corn sheaves into stooks. They all belong somewhere, thought Tom, they all have their place in the world. With his mother gone, he had no place. Would there be somewhere for him in Scrooby? He doubted it, and now with every step he took his hope sank lower.

It was late afternoon. Heat hung in the air, thick and dusty. His shirt stuck to his back and flies buzzed in a cloud about his head. His blistered heels felt painfully raw, and his mouth was dry and parched. Passing a gateway, near which a tall oak spread its branches, he turned in and sank down in the shade. The field gleamed golden with stubble, at its far end a wagon was carrying away its last load of barley sheaves. Long grass grew along the hedgerow, and Tom longed to take off his battered shoes and rest his feet in the coolness.

And there, hidden among the tall grasses, he saw something that made him catch his breath. A basket, covered with a linen cloth against the flies, and beside it a stoppered jug. He raised a corner of the cloth. Bread, cheese, the leg of a fowl, flat oatcakes, a handful of ripe plums. A feast! And just there, waiting to be eaten, as the eggs had been that morning! Surely God had provided for him, as his mother had always urged him to believe, when times were hard. He was ravenous! And thirsty! He picked up the jug, wondering what it contained, pulled out the stopper and sniffed. It smelled like barley beer, or maybe cider. He lifted it to his lips.

"Tha thieving young hound!"

There was a roar, and a cursing, and a sudden swipe across the head that made Tom's head ring and sent the jug spinning out of his hand, spilling brown-gold liquid into the long grass. A man, tall and broad and sweating, in a farmer's smock and breeches, had come through the gateway behind and was standing over Tom, ready to strike again.

"Tek ma dinner, would tha, and me not stopping for bite or sup till now! A good hiding tha needs!"

Tom's heart hammered against his ribs. He raised his arms to protect himself from whatever was to come. He tried to say that he was sorry, that it had been a mistake, but the burly farmer, red-faced, weary, hungry and very angry, was going to listen to no excuses. Tom felt a heavy hand grasp him by the shirt collar, lift him to his feet, shake him like a terrier with a rat, and then drop him, with a kick to his ribs. Tom gasped with pain and rolled over, trying to wriggle away. The man meant to kill him, he was sure.

Then, suddenly, there were drumming hoofbeats, which slowed and paused, and a man's voice saying, "Whoa, now, whoa! What is happening here?"

Two men had dismounted from two tall horses and while one held both bridles the other came to the gateway. He repeated, in a voice that held authority, "What is happening here, fellow? Is this your boy you are beating?"

The farmer straightened up and drew a large red hand across his sweating brow. He said thickly, "Nay, not mine, just some thieving lad after ma dinner." Then, suddenly, he seemed to recognise the man who had stopped. "Why, 'tis Mr Brewster! 'Tis so long since we've seen thee in these parts! Isaac Hooper, sir! Now this lad, he's a stranger here, gipsy no doubt, thieving where he can—"

"Yes, yes." The tall man cut through these explanations with some impatience. "Whoever he is, no need to beat the life out of him. I'm disappointed in you, Isaac. But no doubt you're weary and hungry and thirsty. Go about your business and we'll say no more."

The farmer had his battered hat in his hands now, twirling it in respectful eagerness. "Aye, sir. Thank you, sir. Good to see you again, sir." He gathered up his provisions and was off across the stubble after his wagons, his anger forgotten. The other man called after him "And, Isaac – no need to mention you saw me here today."

"Count on me, sir."

Tom's rescuer sighed, a long and gusty sigh, and said, kindly, "Are you much hurt, lad?"

During their conversation, Tom had been lying curled on his side in the grass, legs drawn up, arms covering his head, hardly daring to breathe. Now he rolled over and looked at the man who had saved him. A tall, broad man in middle age, with bushy brown whiskers turning grey and deep-set grey eyes. He was dressed in dusty cloak and leather boots, with a broad-brimmed hat pulled low over his forehead. Somehow Tom knew he had no need to be afraid of this man. He said, "Not much, thank you, sir," and scrambled to his knees and then to his feet. His ears still rang from the blow he had received, his ribs ached and would doubtless show bruises from the toe of a hard boot. But nothing seemed broken. He swayed a little, from thirst and hunger and weariness. The man called Mr Brewster steadied him, and asked kindly, "Are you thirsty, lad?" and when Tom nodded, he fetched a water bottle from his saddlebag and let him drink as much as he wanted.

The horses, held by the other man, shifted their hooves in the dust as they waited. Their sleek coats were dusty and sweat-streaked from travel, and both horses had bulging leather saddlebags at their sides, with some insignia stamped on them. The other man, his eyes darting uneasily up and down the road, seemed to be growing impatient. He said, "William, we must press on. Time is short, and there is much to be done."

Mr Brewster waved a dismissive hand. "The Lord grants time enough for all we have to do. Now, lad, tell me the reason why you needs must pilfer food from honest working countrymen."

Tom hung his head. He knew he had been wrong to steal. His mother had taught him that, along with the other commandments. He explained, haltingly, about her death, and the instructions she had given to him, and how he had that morning set out upon the road to Scrooby.

The man listened, stroking his short beard. "Scrooby!" he exclaimed. "That is where we are bound for, along with the latest consignment of his majesty's mail."

"Which will be late in arriving, if indeed it arrives at all, and is not stolen by some footpad, should we delay longer and darkness falls," said the other man, who had remounted his horse and seemed increasingly anxious to be off.

Mr Brewster laughed. "Peace, John! Have faith. Well, lad - you have a name, do you not?"

"Tom Turner, sir."

"Well, Tom Turner, as we are all bound alike for Scrooby, I think 'twill be best for us all to travel together. Come, you shall ride behind me."

He lifted Tom with ease and deposited him in the saddle, then swung himself up in front and took the reins.

"Hold on tight to my doublet, Tom Turner. It's but a short ride now to Scrooby on these good mounts they provide for the king's mail. God willing, we'll be there before the lamps are lit."

Chapter Three

The Manor House

It didn't seem too long a distance to Tom, riding pillion on the tall sleek horse with the king's mail on either side of him. He had never ridden horseback before, and clung tight to the belt of the man called William Brewster. In just a short space of time they were entering a village of red-brick, red-roofed houses and soon turning into a road leading to a large house set aside in farmland. In the yard, the men dismounted and Tom was lifted to the ground. Someone came and unbuckled the mail bags, carrying them away, someone else led the horses away to their stabling. Tom heard the whickering of other horses from the stable yard.

By now he felt half dazed with weariness and hunger. He was led to a doorway and then down a dim passage and into a busy, hot and steamy room which seemed to be a kitchen. At any rate, several women and a young girl a little taller than Tom were busy with cooking pots and the chopping of vegetables and stirring of puddings. The smell of stewing meat hung thickly in the air, and Tom's empty stomach groaned afresh. The cooks seemed surprised to see Tom, but when they saw the man with him their faces beamed with astonishment and delight.

"'Tis Master Brewster! Welcome, sir, and God be praised for bringing you again."

Other doors opened, feet came hurrying, voices exclaimed and questioned. Tom found himself squeezed into a corner with a stool to sit on and a trencher of meaty stew in his hands. People entered and left the kitchen, his rescuer was carried off to another room in a hubbub of talk and explanation.

By the time Tom's bowl was empty, his head was drooping and he was half-asleep, overcome by the steamy warmth of the room. Someone took away the empty trencher and then led him to a narrow pallet bed somewhere off the kitchen, where his shoes were removed and a thin blanket was thrown over him. Then he slept.

***

*T*om woke to a rooster crowing outside and the stamp and snorting of horses from the stable yard. Then there came the sound of hooves on cobblestones, which grew fainter and faded away into the distance. Someone had ridden away at first light.

Tom dozed again, and woke to find the young girl, whom he vaguely remembered from the night before, shaking at his shoulder. "Wake up, thou lazy slugabed!

She laughed as she spoke, and he liked the look of her rosy cheeks under a clean white cap. He sat up and fumbled around for his shoes. His muscles were stiff, from the walking, riding and the beating he'd received, but he felt he had rested well.

"What place is this?" he asked the girl, who seemed in no great hurry to get back to her duties.

"Tha's in Scrooby, in t'Manor House," she told him. "Master Brewster brought thee in, don't tha remember? Half asleep, tha was."

"Is this Master Brewster's house?"

"Nay, not any more. He used to be t'postmaster here, years ago, before I were born. Had to go off over the sea, for fear of the king's—"

"Martha!" A shrill voice sounded from the kitchen. "Where art tha, idle lass! Here's t'milk needs skimming, and no water boiling for the hasty pudding!"

"It's Cook, she'll skin me alive!" said Martha, but she couldn't suppress a grin as she scurried off.

Tom fastened his shoes and headed for the outdoors, by a side door off the passage. It was going to be another long hot day. Already the sun was climbing the sky and burning off the early mist that clung to the grass in the enclosed space outside, which he guessed to be a drying-ground from the clothes line strung between two apple trees. A flock of geese just released from their pen were plucking at the grass with a great cackling and hissing. A gateway led through to the stable yard where there was the clatter of horses being fed and watered and their stalls being cleaned. As Tom watched, his rescuer of the night before came striding across the cobbles.

"And how does this morning find you, Tom Turner?" he enquired, with a smile crinkling the corners of his grey eyes.

"Well, thank you, sir." Tom remembered the manners taught by his mother. He had no idea of what was to happen to him now, but as on the day before, this man inspired confidence and hope.

"Good. Well now, I have things to which I must attend, and little time to accomplish them. I leave before light tomorrow, but before then I mean to speak with you on a certain matter. Now, go into the kitchen and tell the cook that Master Brewster says you are to have breakfast.

He strode away across the cobbles towards the stabled horses.

Tom stood for a moment, then turned back to the house, appearing at the kitchen door as the cook was ladling out steaming bowls of porridge from a big pot, and Martha was placing them before a gathering of men breaking their fast around a big table, some on benches and some standing. Nobody took much notice of Tom; there was no room for him to sit, but Martha thrust a steaming bowl into his hands and put down a tankard of sweet buttermilk on the table near him. He ate and drank, listening to the buzz of talk around him. There seemed to be a great deal of excitement that William Brewster was in their midst, though he was aware that once or twice someone would glance sidelong at him and cut short what he was saying. Some kind of secrecy surrounded the visit of Tom's rescuer, and in spite of himself he grew a little anxious as to what it might be.

It was Martha who enlightened him, when breakfast was over and everyone gone about their business for the day. The cook had gone to select a fowl or two from the hen coops for that day's dinner, and Martha was clearing the litter of used mugs and trenchers and gathering bits of bread and blobs of cold porridge for the pig swill bucket. Tom helped by filling the big pots and kettle with fresh water and putting them to heat over the cooking stove. Then there were vegetables to prepare, carrots and onions to chop, apples to be peeled and pastry to mix for pies and puddings. The household obviously had a great many people to feed.

"He's the Separatists' leader, tha knows. Some call him 'The Elder'," said Martha. "Cook says they held their meetings here when he was postmaster. Then the new laws came, that only the king's religion was allowed; any following other beliefs could end up in gaol, or even hanged!" She glanced over her shoulder to see if anyone listened, and dropped her voice. "Master

Brewster was in gaol himself, for a time! Fancy, a good man like him! Then he and some others upped and went, over t'sea, where they could live free of t'king's laws. Now Cook says they're off again, away over t'ocean to t'place they call the New World. Master Brewster came up here, secret like, to wish goodbye to all here before he goes." Her voice lowered again. "None must know; if the king's men caught him—" She drew her fingers across her throat and rolled her eyes dramatically.

"Martha, art 't gossiping again!"

Both children jumped as the plump cook suddenly appeared at the kitchen door, the lifeless forms of two white cockerels dangling from her hands. "I declare t'work will never get done! If thou'rt short of a job, there's these birds to pluck and dress, and floors to scrub!"

Her words were reproving but a twinkle showed in her eye, and she offered them both a raisin pastry before they began on the fowls. The coming of William Brewster seemed to have brought a sense of well-being to the whole household. Stable boys whistled, the cook sang a little song as she wielded a giant rolling pin over the pastry board, and Martha giggled as she and Tom began to make the feathers fly.

All through the day Tom helped as he was told, earning praise from the cook as a 'reet handy, willing lad'. She even said she'd a mind to see if he could stay on as extra help in the kitchen, for the good Lord knew she could do with extra hands, with the post carriers and so many others to feed, and now the meeting-room to make ready at a moment's notice.

"There's to be a meeting here tonight, now Master Brewster's come," said Martha mysteriously.

"What kind of meeting?"

"The kind the Separatists used to have. Still do, only not so regular now, or so often, for fear of being found out. You'll see."

Tom deduced from this that he would be expected to attend the meeting too, and in this he was right. After the evening meal, he found himself part of a large company in one of the big rooms of the Manor House, squeezed in near the doorway with Cook, Martha and the other servants. A buzz of expectation filled the room, which became quiet as the sturdy figure of Master Brewster walked forward to the front.

Tom had been to a church service once or twice, but this was like nothing he had ever seen. Here were no priests in robes and vestments, no incense or bells or processions or chantings. William Brewster greeted the assembly, he spoke a simple prayer of thanksgiving to a God he addressed as his father, he read a passage of Scripture from a well-worn Bible. *"Stand fast therefore in the liberty wherewith Christ hath made us free, and be not entangled again with the yoke of bondage."*

He spoke for a while on this text, and on the freedom offered to all people by trusting in the sacrifice on the cross of the Lord Jesus Christ. Then he spoke of his love for the assembled people, his sadness at leaving them and of the joy and expectation of the hope of freedom to begin life in a new land where all would be free to worship and to pray to God in simplicity and openness. He asked for the prayers of his friends and promised his own prayerful remembrance of them. To Tom's surprise, others then got up and spoke and prayed, some in educated words but most in the simple everyday talk of ordinary country folk. There were exclamations of 'Amen' and 'Praise God' spoken out loud, and many in the meeting had tears in their eyes. Tom felt a warmth rise from this gathering of people that seemed to reach out and enfold him also. He knew now why his mother had urged him to seek out the Separatists.

The meeting had ended, with more tears and embraces and farewells, and Tom was heading for his pallet bed in the kitchen cubbyhole with much to think about, when he felt a hand upon his shoulder.

"A moment, Tom Turner."

William Brewster was on his way to bed too, but now led Tom back into the kitchen and sat down in one of the big oak chairs. He leaned forward, looking steadily into Tom's eyes as the boy stood before him.

"Tom, from what you tell me, you are quite alone in the world. Now, I have no doubt I could find a home for you here among the good people of Scrooby. Yet, maybe, God has something even better in store for you. I've prayed much, and I feel that he would have you come voyaging with me, to sail on the good ship *Mayflower* to the New World and a new life. What do you think, Tom?"

Tom felt his mouth drop open in amazement. His thoughts whirled. All day long he had been kept busy with one thing and another, hardly having a moment to think about what would happen on the next day, or the day after that.

William Brewster leant forward and patted him kindly on the shoulder. "I see you're overwhelmed with my suggestion. Tired out too. Go to bed now, Tom. But think on what I've said. It could be that this is God's good plan for you. Come the morning, we'll speak again."

Chapter Four

Stay or go?

Tom lay tossing and turning upon his pallet bed. Around him the big house was silent, the very walls themselves seeming to be quietly breathing as they slumbered. Tom was tired out, aching in every limb from the various activities of the past few days, his thoughts whirling as he tried to make sense of it all.

He did not know what to make of the offer that William Brewster had made to him, the promise of a new life in a new land. His whole life had been spent in the streets of his home town, happily at first, then spiralling downward into desperate need and misery, and finally, heartbreak and the frightening awareness that he was quite alone.

This man had offered him the chance of people around him again, kindly, hardworking people, and maybe, somewhere in the future, a chance of happiness. But it all seemed unreal, like a morning mist that might melt away and vanish as if it had never been. He couldn't imagine a tall ship, or a vast ocean. He could not picture the new land that William Brewster had tried to describe to him. His head ached, the blanket was knotted and twisted from his restless turnings. How could he come to a decision as he had been asked?

He couldn't. That much was clear at least. He would have no answer to give when it was asked of him. It was all too much. He thought of his mother, lying in that cold grave in a neglected place. A sob rose in his throat. He flung off the blanket and searched about for his boots. He must go.

A new suit of clothing had been provided for him, warm knitted stockings, stout boots, a jerkin and breeches of good woollen cloth. He hesitated – would it be stealing to take these clothes? He had no choice really. His grimy and tattered old garments had been gathered up and taken away somewhere, possibly to the garden bonfire. He pulled on his boots and outer clothes and quietly made his way to the back door, gently pulling back the bolts so that they did not squeak.

A silvery moonlight lit the cobblestones and outlined the tall oaks and beeches around the yard. Beyond lay open fields, glittering with a covering of dew. Tom headed across the first one, making for the cover of a dark tangle of woodland in the distance. Where he would go he had no clear idea. He just knew that he could not face the kindly eyes of William Brewster, could not frame an answer to the question he would be asked. He wanted to hide, to run, he wanted things to be as they were when he had a family. He wanted his mother.

Sobs rose in his throat and tears ran down his cheeks. By the time he reached the woodland he was so overcome with grief and weariness that he thought his legs would carry him no further. For a while he stumbled on, crashing through undergrowth, feeling brambles tear at his legs and hardly noticing when a slim stem of elder whipped across his cheek. Sobs racked his body. Suddenly his foot caught against a root from a tall beech tree and he fell to his knees. He had no will left to pull himself to his feet again. No will to go on, or really any will to live. He curled himself up on a carpet of beech mast and fallen leaves under the tree and sobbed until he fell asleep.

Tom awoke with a start. He was cramped and shivering. A cold morning light was beginning to filter through the trees. Small birds were twittering in the branches and pecking at ripening blackberries and rose-hips in the undergrowth. And someone was coming – he could hear a crackling of small twigs breaking under booted feet.

Tom had no energy left to run. He sat up and huddled against the smooth beech trunk, and next moment the broad figure of William Brewster, hat pulled down over his forehead, came into view.

He stopped and looked at Tom in silence for a moment, leaning on his stout hazel stick. Tom hung his head, confused and ashamed. He was shivering with the morning chill and his clothes were damp with dew. The Elder spoke after a moment. "Come, Tom. Let us go home to breakfast."

He held out his hand and helped Tom to his feet. Dazed and shivering, Tom followed as he began to retrace his steps through the trees. Elder Brewster asked for no explanations. He made no rebuke. He seemed only glad that he had found the boy and began to talk gently as they made their way out of the woodland. "I asked too much of you, too soon, Tom. I see that now. I pray that you will forgive me, and allow yourself all the time you need to make your decision."

Tom felt his breath catch in his throat. He had expected at least some rebuke for his ingratitude, some punishment, even. And this man was asking him for forgiveness! He could not answer. All he could say was "How – how did you find me?"

William Brewster laughed and swung his stick to hold back a prickly spray of bramble. "Easily enough! You left a trail in the dew as plain as a stampeding bullock!"

He laughed again, and suddenly a heavy weight seemed to lift from somewhere deep inside Tom. Emerging from the trees, they saw the early morning mist begin to rise like smoke from the grass, and the first rays of sun break through. With the coming of morning, the confusion and fear and sorrow were beginning to melt away like the mist. He knew now what his answer to this man must be.

***

*T*wo days later they were on the road before the rooster crowed, William Brewster and Tom Turner, on the back of one of the well-cared-for horses kept for the delivery of King James's mail, and travelling at a fair clip towards the south.

Tom still felt a little breathless at this turn of events, but he had rested and eaten well over the past days and his spirits had risen. This was a new day and a new adventure.

For a time they travelled fast, the horse's hooves clickety-clacking on the wide road, the sun rising overhead. Then their pace slowed, to give relief to the horse for a spell. William Brewster could talk now, without his words being snatched away before they reached Tom's ears.

"We should be in Plymouth by Friday night," he said. "By God's grace, the fitting of the ship, its provisioning and the assembling of all who mean to sail in her should be almost complete. We hope to sail shortly after my return. Hast thou been aboard ship before, Tom?"

"No", said Tom. He had never even seen the sea, couldn't imagine any body of water so vast and so lonely as it must be, or that a ship could sail on it from continent to continent. He listened with rapt attention as William Brewster talked, telling of the rigging and the sails and the various decks of the *Mayflower*, things that were all a mystery to Tom. He told of the Separatists' journey to Holland, of the years spent in the Dutch city of Leyden, of the decision to travel further into new and uncharted lands. He said that some weeks earlier this same summer they had set out, together with a smaller ship called the *Speedwell*, only to be obliged to return when the *Speedwell* proved unseaworthy.

"Some are uneasy to be sailing so late in the year, with a two-month voyage ahead and winter weather on its way," he said, flicking away the flies that began to cluster around the head of their mount. "But we have to believe that God's timing is always best. For example, the delay gave me the chance to bid my farewells to those I love and leave behind in the north. And it gave you the chance of a new life when you have need of it."

He reined in the horse to a halt, to allow them both to dismount so that they could refresh themselves and allow the horse to drink too. Tom noticed that they stopped only in lonely places, and quickly drew aside into a lane or a byway, away from the eyes of other travellers.

"I still have a price on my head," he said with a laugh, offering Tom a draught from his water bottle. "King James and his men would show me short shrift if I fell into their hands. And all for daring to worship freely, and lead others in doing so. We live in strange times, Tom. But, God willing, our new life in a new land will offer opportunities such as we've never dreamed."

Handing back the water bottle, Tom felt his heart give a little skip of excitement. Life had been hard for him of late, hard and dull and full of heartbreak. Who knew what the future might have in store?

They continued on their way, stopping at dusk at a place where they could rest overnight and where there would be a fresh horse available for the next day's mail. Master Brewster knew the places where he was known and trusted and was careful to stop only at those villages or inns. In between, nobody questioned the Royal Insignia or the man who carried it on his saddlebags, apparently travelling with his young son as companion.

Tom had never realised that his own country was so large, so beautiful and so diverse. They travelled over lonely mountain roads, through leafy tree-lined parkland with cows grazing and fields of ripe corn, over narrow river bridges and through thick forests where the horse's hooves were muffled on thick leaf mould and the wind sighed in tall treetops. Their direction was to the south and west. In all the farmlands, harvest was in full swing, wagons groaning under loads of sheaves, stubble gleaming gold or already being ploughed for next year's crops by teams of straining carthorses and sweating ploughmen. Flocks of white gulls screamed around the turned furrows, searching for exposed grubs and insects.

William Brewster pointed out to Tom interesting sights as they came into view – an ancient turreted castle here, a slim church spire there, the chimney smoke from a village nestled into a fold of hills. He talked about the different types of soil – the dark peaty earth of bogs and moors, rich red clay of fertile farmland, light sandy soil that showed the coast was not far away. He pondered on the land that awaited them in the New World – rich and fertile, with a mild climate and abundant growth, or so the word had come from those already settled in the place they called Virginia.

One afternoon they were overtaken by another traveller, riding hard in the same direction as themselves. He reined in beside them, giving the man and boy a keen look. As his horse danced impatiently, anxious to be off again, the man said, "Friend, if you be who I think you be, you had better seek cover. The king's men ride this way!"

And he was off again in a clatter of hooves before he could be thanked. William Brewster sprang into action, urging forward his own mount, to whom he had been giving a short respite by slowing almost to a walk. Tom clung on tightly as they rode at a gallop towards a patch of woodland through which they must pass. Once within the trees, Elder Brewster swung suddenly aside into their shelter, pressing deep into the forest of tall trunks. Some of the oaks and beeches still had their leaves of russet and yellow and brown, sheltering them from the road. Away from the road, William swung to the ground and motioned Tom to do the same. Then he took the bridle and led them deeper, their footfalls muffled by soft leaf mould. Suddenly, fast travelling hoofbeats came clattering along the road they had turned from. William put his finger to his lips and held the horse still, motioning to Tom not to move.

Tom held his breath and waited for the hoofbeats to pass. Instead, they slowed and then stopped at the fringe of the woodland. Men's voices sounded, close enough for the odd word or two to be heard. "Taken to the woods, you think," he heard one say. Some of the others seemed to disagree. One said that they were wasting time and letting the fox get well ahead of them. "Aye, but a fox is a wily crittur," said the first. "He'll find cover and sit there laughing."

"Flush him out then?" said a fresh voice. Tom guessed there were five or six men. His heart was thumping. But one of the others said, "Ride on, I say."

Their horses' hooves skittered and scraped on the road's surface as they talked. Then one of the horses tossed its head with a clinking of its bridle and gave a shrill whinny. Tom saw their own horse's ears prick forward and its head go up. In a moment it would let out an answering whinny and their hiding place would be discovered.

But William Brewster's hand was steady on the bridle, keeping the horse's head still. With his other hand he stroked its neck, gentling it, whispering soothingly into the twitching ears. The horse stood quietly again, and Tom let out his breath.

After a few more moments, the king's men seemed to decide that it was better to ride on than begin to search the woodland. They rode on at a gallop until the only sounds again were the wind in the treetops and the gentle snorting of the horse. Tom and William Brewster looked at each other.

"I low did you do that? Make the horse stay quiet?" asked Tom shakily.

The Elder smiled. "I saw enough of horses while I was postmaster to understand them a little, I think," he said. "But it's the Lord we must thank, my boy. Now, we must take extra care. It seems to be known that we are upon the road. I think we will stay off the main highway and take to the smaller lanes and byways. God be thanked we are not far from our destination."

This vigilance meant that extra hours were added to the journey, but in another day they had reached white chalky soil on gently swelling downs and fields that gleamed white in the afternoon sun. "One more day and we shall reach journey's end," said William Brewster, with renewed good cheer in his voice. Even that day's mount seemed to feel new confidence, flicking his ears forward and seeming to increase his stride. By the end of the next day they were travelling gently downhill, leaving behind rich farmland and heading for a town that straggled along the seashore with, behind it, a shimmering line of blue that could have been sky but, Tom suddenly realised, was not. Above their heads, seagulls swooped and screamed, and there was a strong taste of salt upon his lips. A small white sail showed on the blue near the shore, and then another and another, and Tom realised that for the first time in his life he was seeing the sea.

Chapter Five

Plymouth

The town of Plymouth stood at a place where two rivers met the sea, with high cliffs looking down over the sparkling waters of the Sound. It was busier and more bustling than any place Tom had seen before, and he looked about him in wonder as William Brewster led him through the streets down to the West Quay, where the ship lay at anchor. They were on foot now, having left the horse and saddlebags at the last mailing post among trusted friends who had wished them a heartfelt Godspeed.

A fresh wind blew from the sea, and the water seemed to glitter like blue-green glass with white-topped waves breaking the surface. Craft bobbed in the harbour and sea birds whirled and screamed overhead. Tom thought he had never seen anything as wonderful as this vast ocean and would have liked time to stand and gaze, but the Separatist leader hurried him on.

As dusk fell they reached the harbour, lined with tall buildings and warehouses stretching almost down to the water's edge. A great bustle of activity was taking place in and around the buildings and on the quayside. Goods were being loaded into boats and ferried to one of the tall ships in the Sound, while seamen in stocking caps hurried about their business. Tom saw that some of the busy men wore the plain doublets and breeches of the Separatists, with wide-brimmed hats and white linen at the neck. Master Brewster hurried him into one of the tall buildings and down steps to a cool, dim, cellar-like room, where a number of people, women and children as well as men, seemed to be making ready for a journey. Bundles of clothing and household goods, pots and pans, bedding and even boxes of books were being carried up the steps and onto the quayside, amid a quiet hum of conversation. All of the people greeted William Brewster with joy and a touch of relief, as though there had been a hint of doubt that he would return safely. He returned their greetings and led Tom to where a brown-haired, kind-faced woman was ladling hot food from a cooking pan over a brazier and handing bowls to a large group of children gathered around her.

"Mary, here is one more for your good bean porridge," he said, laying his hand on Tom's shoulder. "He lost his mother not two weeks ago and will sail with us. One more will make no odds. Tom, this is my good wife and two of these rascals are my sons."

He disappeared into the crowd, and Tom found himself surrounded by the curious eyes of several children, boys and girls of all ages. Mary Brewster seemed kind but very busy. There was no time for polite conversation. She gave him food and drink and showed him a place to sleep on the crowded floor among the bundles and baskets, sharing blankets with her own sons. He thought it would be impossible to sleep, on a hard floor in a strange place, with a buzz of voices and constant movement all around, but he was asleep in minutes, worn out from the long day's journeying.

Tom awoke to daylight glinting in through dusty small windows and a renewed bustle of activity around him. Maybe some of the people had not slept at all but had gone on with their packing and preparation all through the night. The elder of the two Brewster boys was tugging at his elbow. "Wake up! Today we're going to sail!"

A sense of anticipation was in the air. The warehouse room was rapidly being emptied of its chests and baskets and bundles, as the last of them were carried out to the quayside. From the quay came the shouts of seamen and the splash of oars. Someone thrust bread and cheese into Tom's hand, and he followed the others out into the morning.

The *Mayflower* stood at anchor in the Sound, rocking a little in a gentle swell, while small boats plied to and fro taking the stuff to the ship. Tom stood with the wind ruffling his hair and looked in amazement at the vessel. It seemed huge to him, though William Brewster had told him that the *Mayflower* was not a very large sailing ship. Three tall masts with furled sails pointed to the sky, with a bowsprit slanting from the beakhead, and already sailors were climbing among the rigging. He could not imagine being on board such a ship himself.

"We sailed from Holland," said the elder Brewster boy, showing off a little. "Wrestling was sick, but not me. I've got my sea legs!"

He had a merry face, with grey eyes like his father's, and was probably a year or two younger than Tom. Tom thought that the younger Brewster brother had a very strange name, but couldn't believe his ears when he heard what the older boy was called. Love! He had never before heard a boy called by such a strange and embarrassing name. But he'd noticed already, from mothers calling to their children, that many of the Separatists' children had peculiar names – Resolved, Humility, Remember. They were strange and unusual people altogether. But he felt safe with them, safe, and somehow cared for, despite the haste and hustle, as though he truly mattered.

The Pilgrims, men bareheaded in the morning breeze, gathered on the quayside and sang, prayed and read Scriptures, while the gulls screamed and dipped about their heads. Their voices sounded sweet and harmonious out here in the open, accompanied by the splashing of wavelets. Tom noticed that there were other travellers waiting to board the *Mayflower*, some with wives and children, who listened respectfully to the worship though they stood apart and did not join in.

"They're called the Strangers," whispered Love Brewster at his elbow. "They'll be with us on the ship. And the soldiers will be there too."

Tom had seen the company of military men, under the direction of a short, stocky, red-haired captain, march smartly to the quay, the sun glinting on their helmets and armour. They stood stiffly to attention while they waited.

Then the small boats were being held steady while the passengers began to board them, the men helping the women and children. The others watched as the first boatloads were rowed out to the ship. Tom got into a boat with the Brewster family and some others, squinting against the sun as he watched the ship loom nearer and nearer, until they were close to its side where a rope ladder waited for them to climb aboard.

A young crew member stood at the top of the ladder, helping the women and children onto the deck. He took Tom's hand with a firm grip and heaved him safely on board. Tom looked up into laughing blue eyes in a tanned face, and a thatch of fair hair curling from under a seaman's green stocking cap.

"Steady now, young sir," he said, clapping Tom on the shoulder. "You'll soon get used to the swell," he added, as Tom felt the deck sway under his feet and grabbed at the rail. "By the time we make landfall, you'll be up in the rigging like a monkey."

Tom felt himself pulled by Love Brewster along the unsteady deck towards the companionway, down which the rest of the family was disappearing into the depths of the ship. Love had taken upon himself the task of guide and instructor to Tom, which gave him a feeling of importance.

"That's John Alden," he said. "He joined the crew at Plymouth. He's the ship's cooper. You know what a cooper is? It's someone who makes barrels and casks, and mends them when they get leaky."

Tom didn't reply. He knew exactly what a cooper was, had watched his father at work many times. He had seen how skilfully he bent the wooden staves and rounded off the ends with his hand adze, how carefully the metal bindings were fitted, what pride his father had taken in the casks he had produced, the butterchurns and hogsheads, the firkins and buckets and washtubs.

It gave him a strange sick feeling to be reminded of his father. But whether he was alive or dead, it made no difference now. He would never see him again.

Below decks, there was a confusion of milling bodies and questioning voices as each family sought to fit themselves and their personal belongings into the allocated spaces. Each family had what was called a 'cabin', but it was really nothing more than a small space little larger than a bed, with thin plywood divisions on only some of the sides. Already the women were shaking out blankets and rigging them up on ropes to provide a little more privacy. Tom was told that he would be sharing with the Brewster family and another boy called Richard More whom they had also taken into their care. Richard had a brother and sister on board, each placed with one of the other families. Several of the families seemed to have an extra child or two with them who was not their own. It did not look like being the most comfortable of journeys.

"Let's go on deck," said one of the bigger boys, Samuel Fuller. Most of the harassed mothers were glad to have their restless sons out from under their feet, if only to give them a chance to stow away their baskets and bundles wherever they could find space.

A busy scene met them on the main deck. Groups of men milled about, the sailors going about their duties, while the Pilgrims and other travellers talked together in groups. The military men with their captain stood stiffly apart, as though already waiting for some action. Tom saw two dogs, a mastiff and a spaniel, on chains with one of the travellers, sniffing at the strange scents and bracing themselves awkwardly against the motion of the ship. A nervous cackling came from a wooden crate of chickens bound for the New World. High above, the furled sails gleamed white against the rigging. Looking back at the quayside, it already seemed far away, the people there tiny, bustling, toy-like figures, like puppets on a stage.

Love Brewster pointed to a man standing near the ladder to the quarterdeck. "That's the ship's Captain. Christopher Jones is his name. And that tall man with him is Master Bradford. He's one of our leaders and a great friend of my father. And that man over there—"

He was interrupted by a swarthy, scowling seaman with a red bandanna around his head, carrying a keg on his shoulder, who pushed his way roughly through the group of boys, causing little Wrestling to stumble and fall. "Watch out, you Separatist pups! Stay below decks where you belong, can't you?"

He disappeared below with a curse. One of the bigger boys helped Wrestling to his feet. The others looked at one another. They were used to strict parents who demanded obedience, but not rough treatment and curses. Samuel Fuller pulled a face at the retreating back of the seaman and they all laughed, a little anxiously.

"Is it nearly dinner time?" wondered Love. "I'm starving."

Food was cooked by the women over small braziers in the confines of the travellers' quarters, the braziers standing in trays of sand to steady them. Even so, the arrangement seemed hazardous. One stumbling body, unstable from the lurching of the ship, or someone carelessly allowing their skirts to brush against the brazier, could cause fire that might be in danger of setting the whole ship alight. There was a bigger stove in the forecastle, but far too many people for all to take a turn. Often there would be long waits for meals; the children would soon learn how pointless it was to expect food whenever they were hungry.

But on this first day, spirits were high and everything an exciting novelty. They ate good mutton stew and fresh bread, and afterwards played on deck until a sudden activity among the crew showed that something was happening. Men climbed the rigging, the anchor was raised by the turning of the windlass, the sails were loosed and flapped in the breeze. The wind was strengthening and the tide turning. They would soon sail.

Chapter Six

At sea

The *Mayflower* sailed on the evening tide. Tom, with some of the other children, stood at the rails of the top deck and watched the town of Plymouth grow smaller and smaller as the ship sailed into the rays of the setting sun. Then they were ordered below to the crowded quarters of the Pilgrims, to listen to the evening prayers and afterwards go to bed for their first night on ship. Tom found himself crammed into a small space at the foot of the Brewsters' rough wooden bunk, sharing a thin pallet on the floor with Love Brewster and Richard More. All around him were the sighings and snorings and talk in low voices from the other families settling in for the night, with the occasional whimper of a small child or thump as someone turned over in their confined space. He thought he would not sleep a wink, but the rocking motion of the ship was strangely soothing and, before he knew it, the night had passed and a half-light was seeping in between decks.

Tom tried to roll over and heard a muffled "Ow!" as his elbow dug into Love Brewster's side. The younger boy sat up, rubbing his eyes, and then Richard More's head appeared too, tousled and bleary-eyed. So limited was their sleeping space that if one woke and stirred, so did the others.

The bunk bed was empty, the Brewster parents and 4-year-old Wrestling gone. The sound of a hymn being sung filtered down from the deck above. The Pilgrims were conducting their morning prayers out under the open sky.

Love grinned. "They let us off prayers this morning," he said, and scrambled to his feet. "But you can be sure it won't happen again. Let's go up on deck."

Out on deck, away from the dim stuffy quarters, the world was fresh and sun-washed, a good following wind filling the sails. Tom stood for a moment getting his sea legs and listening to the creak of timbers, the snapping of the sails and the wind thrumming in the rigging. Near the rails, the Separatists, heads bowed, were being led in prayer by William Brewster. Sailors went about their work, some grinning at the sight of this gathering. Tom saw the fair head of John Alden passing on his way below decks; the young cooper seemed to remember him and gave him a wave. At the other end of the deck Miles Standish was drilling his men, strutting down the line like a short, stocky bulldog, his red hair covered by his helmet. Tom had overheard one of the women say to another that he had a fearsome temper, but that his wife Rose knew just how to manage him; she was travelling with him and was the sweetest person, just like her name.

Tom was beginning to recognise some of the other travellers, and to put names to faces. There were Master and Mistress Mullins, who had a son about Tom's age and a very pretty older daughter. The Allerton family had several children, boys and girls, and there were the Fullers with their son Samuel. Among the Strangers, Master and Mistress Billington had brought their two sons, older boys than Tom, and very bold and mischievous-looking.

"Those two may prove a handful!" Tom had heard Mary Brewster remark privately to her husband, and William had nodded agreement. "Though I do not doubt it will be something of a trial to all the boys here, confined as they are," he added.

Tom felt his spirits beginning to rise. Already the sadness of the last weeks was beginning to fade a little. This new life of freedom and fresh air and a new start seemed suddenly a wonderful adventure, and even the dull rations of pease pudding and bean soup and salt meat would only be for a short time. With the other boys he explored the ship, scrambling up and down ladders, peering through hatches, looking into the hold where the food, the tools they would need for the new land, supplies to last the first months and all the other necessities of life were stored, together with the soldiers' weaponry and several kegs of gunpowder.

"If we had a pinch of that, we could make ourselves a fine bang," said John Billington, the older of the two brothers, his dark eyes gleaming. The others discussed this possibility with some interest. Most of the boys would have loved to act on this idea, if they thought they'd get away without punishment. But nothing would go unnoticed in the confined spaces of a sailing ship. And just then the unpleasant sailor in the red bandanna, who seemed to have taken a strong dislike to all the travellers, came by. He grinned at them, but it was not a pleasant grin. "And what do you think you're poking your noses into now?"

"Nothing," said Samuel Fuller quickly.

John Billington stood his ground. "And what's it to you, anyway?"

The sailor stopped grinning. He came closer and reached out a wiry hand to grip John's coat collar. "What's that you said?"

Tom felt his heart begin to thump hard. They were on their own down here, no adult from the Separatists or Strangers to call upon for help. And this man, Jack Fry, had a glint in his eye that was cruel as well as bullying. He pushed his face close to John's, twisting the boy's collar so that he began to gasp for breath. John was a big boy, tall and well-grown for his age, but he was no match for the hard hands and muscular strength of the seaman. "See here, Separatist scum! Jack Fry stands no lip from the likes of you! You've riled me now, the whole bunch of you! Stay out of my way, if you want to get to your New World, which I doubt you'll reach anyhow!"

He let John go, thrusting him hard against the wooden kegs. John picked himself up, rubbing his neck where a red weal was beginning to show. "Filthy pig!" he muttered. But all of the boys watched the seaman's heels disappear up the ladder with a profound sense of relief, and a resolution to avoid him like plague in the future.

After a few days, a change came. Overnight the blue skies and gentle motion of the ship turned to strong winds and rough seas that sent the ship pitching and rolling, huge waves seeming to rise up and threaten to engulf the decks. Thrilled, the boys clung to the rails and felt the deck heave and shudder under their feet. This was a real adventure! But suddenly, Tom felt his stomach seeming to heave too, in time with the waves. Next moment he was vomiting over the rails.

He wiped his streaming eyes and saw that several of the other boys' faces had turned a strange greenish shade too. Then suddenly John Alden was there, urging them away from the rails and across the heaving deck to the companionway.

"Get below, boys, lie down and stay still. That's the only thing you can do with seasickness. And wait. It'll pass."

When the boys stumbled down the ladder to the travellers' quarters, they were greeted on all sides by groans, heavings and splutterings. Many of the travellers lay prostrate on their beds, moving only to vomit painfully into a bucket on the floor. Only a few hardier souls seemed immune. These were soon kept busy, emptying the buckets over the side, mopping up spills, tending to the small children, fetching water and holding heads for the afflicted ones to take a sip.

Beneath them the ship bucked and plunged and ploughed through the waves. The smell and stuffiness of their cramped quarters seemed unbearable. Tom lay down on his tiny pallet, with Love and Richard groaning on either side of him. His head throbbed and his stomach, long emptied of that morning's breakfast, continued to heave. Someone offered him a sip of water and he tried to thank them, but instead had to dive for the nearest bucket again. He thought he would surely die, and wondered with a kind of vague curiosity whether it would hurt much.

Then, on the third day, Tom woke from a fitful doze to find that he was thirsty and, even more strangely, hungry too. He raised his head cautiously. No nausea, no need to rush for the bucket.

The sea had calmed. Could he be better? He got up carefully, a little light-headed and wobbly in the legs, but not sick any more, and knew that he was better. Around him, one or two others were getting up or sitting weakly on the edges of their bunks. Many still lay white and ill. William Brewster had risen and gone on deck, and now he reappeared with water for his wife and boys.

"Ah, Tom. God be thanked, you're mending," he said, his eyes lighting in a face that still looked grey and sunken. "Get some air, and then give a hand where you can. There's many still can't help themselves. Here, take a drink."

Tom drank, and managed to nibble a little of the hard biscuit from the supplies. Still a little shaky, he climbed the ladder to the main deck. The sea was somewhat calmer now, and with great relief he stood by the top of the ladder, breathing in the cool, fresh salt air.

Next moment he was almost knocked over as Jack Fry came striding past with a coil of rope in his hands. Tom made to turn away, but the man stopped and barred his way. He gave a sneering look at the boy's pale face. "Still alive then, Separatist brat? Only just though, by the looks of you. Not so high and holy now, eh?"

Tom said nothing. He wondered why this man hated the Pilgrims so much, when they were such kind and gentle people. Since their encounter near the gunpowder keg, Jack Fry had missed no chance to sneer at the boys, and the rest of the travellers, except for the soldiers. Those he did not dare to address. The boys avoided him whenever they could, but it was not always possible on the confines of a sailing ship. Several of them had suffered from a sly tweak, or a cuff round the ear, or a shove that sent them reeling across the deck, whenever there were no witnesses. One day he had slyly tripped Richard More and sent him tumbling down the companionway steps. Mary Brewster had remarked on the bruises the next day. But none of the boys breathed a word, fearing that worse things would happen if they did.

Tom said nothing, keeping his eyes down, and hoped that Jack Fry would soon go on his way, but the man seemed inclined to linger, idly swinging the rope end in his hands. From the corner of his eye Tom could see that Miles Standish was on deck with some of his men, and breathed a little easier. There'd be less chance of bullying with the soldiers about. But Jack Fry could not resist the chance of some verbal harassment.

"No doubt many of you won't last the journey. Then we'll have the pleasure of dropping you overboard one after another to feed the fishes." He laughed and added, "And then we'll share out your goods between us, all your pans and kettles and books and fancy fal-lals."

He gave an unpleasant laugh. Tom had the feeling he was not joking. He was feeling shaky again and beginning to sweat.

Next moment, Captain Miles Standish came striding along the deck, and the seaman quickly took himself off down the ladder.

"Are ye feeling stronger, lad?" enquired the Captain, pausing to look at the boy.

"Yes, thank you, sir."

Captain Standish nodded and patted his shoulder briskly. "Good. You'll do well now. And what might be your name?"

"Tom, sir. Tom Turner."

"Tom Turner. Well, Tom, I must be about my business. And pay no mind to that bullying braggart Jack Fry. He'll meet his just deserts, no doubt."

So the Captain had noticed the taunts and jeers that had been directed to the Pilgrims by the man in the red bandanna. His words proved more prophetic than he could have known. Two days later, as the passengers emerged one by one from below, weak but recovering, the seaman Jack Fry suddenly sickened of some unknown malady and within another day was dead. All of them watched as his body, wrapped in sailcloth, was committed to the sea. It sank without trace.

There were those among the Separatists who gave thanks, considering that the justice of God had fallen upon their tormentor. One of the boys discovered Jack's red bandanna caught in a part of the rigging and fastened it on the rail to flap in the breeze.

"If we had one of the soldier's muskets," said John Billington, eyeing a couple of the military men across the deck, "we could take pot shots at it. Jack liked to hurt us and make fun of us. But we're the ones having the last laugh."

None of them had much hope that Captain Standish or his men would lend a musket and ammunition. Nor were there any stones for throwing. Then one of the boys produced a dish of cold porridge, left over from someone's breakfast, and for a while they contented themselves with throwing blobs of it at the flapping red cloth. Seagulls swooped low and grabbed at the food, until they attracted the attention of Mary Brewster, who had come to take the air on deck. She hurried over to the group of boys.

"What is this – the thoughtless wasting of good food?"

John Billington explained that they were only showing their contempt for the dead sailor and their joy that he had gone.

Mistress Brewster looked stern. "Stop this, immediately. For one thing, such waste is intolerable. We may have been glad of that food before the voyage is over."

Tom had noticed that when the boys were together they were not always as respectful as when they were with their families. Now Love looked cheekily at his mother and said boldly, "Even cold, lumpy porridge?"

"Even that, unmannerly, ungrateful child! Would your father to hear that remark, be sure you would be soundly chastised!"

"We had nothing else to throw," said Richard More. "And we are so glad Jack is dead and can torment us no longer. The elders praised God for it in their prayers this morning."

Mary Brewster's face grew thoughtful and saddened. She watched for a moment the waves washing the sides of the ship. "As to that, I somewhat fear that we are forgetting God's mercy when we so quickly turn to rejoicing," she said quietly. "God may or may not have seen fit to mete out swift punishment. But we must never forget the words of our Saviour, who said that all have sinned, and therefore all stand in need of mercy and forgiveness. We must remember that for that reason he died upon the cross."

The group of boys was silent. They were used to the men's discourse and teaching of the Scriptures, but the women did not often speak like this.

"You mean – a bully like Jack could find God's mercy too?" asked Love disbelievingly.

"Surely, if he sought it. The Scriptures say our Lord came not for the righteous, but to call sinners to repentance," said Mistress Brewster, and added, "He forgives us much. Let us also have forgiving hearts."

She untied the red bandanna and dropped it over the rail, where it floated for a moment on the waves and then was gone. "Come," she said. "You, Love, and Richard and Tom. I can find tasks to occupy you. And you others – I doubt not that your families would thank you for some help. Satan will always find mischief for idle hands to do."

Chapter Seven

Landfall!

The *Mayflower* boys were in trouble again. Early that morning, after prayers and breakfast, they had been sent above to make room for the activities of the women and smaller children below. They were glad to go; the quarters of the travellers had quickly become stuffy, airless and stinking with the smells of unwashed bodies, unwashed clothing, cooking and babies. They were also dark and overcrowded.

Up on deck, the air was fresh. It was colder, a stiff wind blew and the ship rocked and swayed, its sails billowing and snapping above them. But the presence of the boys seemed no more welcome. When they hung around the rigging, eyeing the nimble sailors who clambered about it like monkeys and wondering if they could do the same, they were chased away by an irritated seaman who said he had enough to do without scraping up fallen bodies from the deck. The soldiers muttered about the need for discipline, and their Captain seemed in a bad mood. It was useless to offer to walk the two dogs around the deck; last time they did this the dogs had broken loose and chased the ship's skinny cat up one of the masts, where it clung for hours spitting and snarling while the dogs barked below. When one of the smaller boys poked a mop handle into the chicken coop, the squawking and clucking brought Mistress Chilton, red-faced and fuming, up the ladder from below. Those fowls were to provide eggs in the New World, she scolded, and at this rate they would go off the lay for months. Everyone was busy, above decks and below. The boys drifted from stem to stern, from deck to deck, in search of occupation.

It was Joseph Mullins who noticed that the hatch to the hold was slightly open, wide enough for a boy to squeeze through. John Billington's eyes gleamed. As well as provisions, tools and supplies, the hold held the weaponry and ammunition that drew him like a magnet.

"Some of you keep watch," he said. "Francis, you and I will go down and see what we can see."

The boys clustered around the ladder, half admiring and half fearful, and watched John and Francis squeeze through the space. There was a shuffling and scrambling from the musty dimness below. The other boys waited uneasily, nervous of what might happen if they were discovered. But the rest of the ship was occupied about its own business. Samuel called down into the darkness, "What are you doing?"

There was no reply, except for more shuffling and a muffled clattering.

"John!" called Samuel. "Are you coming up soon?"

Again no reply. Then suddenly, a loud report rang out, a thud and a clatter, and next moment the scared white faces of the Billington brothers appeared through the hatch. "Quick! Pull us up!"

They were yanking the two from the hatch when a clattering of boots sounded on the ladder, and Captain Standish was there, red and furious, roaring like a mad bull.

"Ye meddling young divils! What have ye done now?"

He grasped the two offenders by their shirt collars and hauled them up the ladder. The others followed, guilty and trembling, and listened in silence as the Captain demanded explanations. It seemed that John had discovered a musket, loaded it and loosed it off, maybe more by accident than by design. Fortunately the bullet had embedded itself in a bale of blankets.

The Captain looked as though he would burst with rage and shook the boys as a terrier shakes a rat. He said they could count themselves fortunate, considering the amount of gunpowder down there, that the whole ship had not blown sky high and dispatched them all to kingdom come. They deserved to be flayed alive, he said, but they were the responsibility of their own parents and so would be delivered to them for suitable chastisement. And they would never, never, venture near the baggage hold again, on pain of death.

The boys were duly delivered to their respective families, John and Francis and the other Strangers to their cabins, where whacks and yells soon told of the nature of their punishment. The Separatist parents could deal out chastisement of this nature too, when need be, but this time it was also felt that the boys must be made to dwell at length on the serious nature of their crime.

William Brewster collected all the boys together and faced them sternly.

"I know it is the nature of boys to be curious, to meddle, to try out new things, especially when we are all unnaturally confined and lacking in exercise and useful employment," he said gravely, his grey eyes seeking out each face in turn. Tom hung his head and felt his cheeks redden with shame. Beside him, he felt the others shift uncomfortably. The discomfort grew as the Elder went on, "But with this morning's escapade, the lives of all on board could have been in jeopardy. One stray spark lodging in a keg of gunpowder and—" He paused, leaving the results to their imaginations, and then went on. "It's only by the grace of God that such a calamity was avoided. I am hard put to devise a punishment that will suitably impress you with the seriousness of your actions. I think it best that you meditate long and well on your folly, while at the same time taking in and digesting portions of Scripture that will serve to cleanse, nourish and build up that inner strength of character you stand so sadly in need of. As indeed, do we all."

Following this homily, he assigned long passages of Scripture to each boy, fitted to their age and ability, and said that they would be confined to their own cabins for the rest of the day while absorbing these. He and others would test them at intervals, pray with them and look for signs of genuine repentance. They would also forfeit the noon meal.

So it was that Tom, with Love and Richard, found himself sitting disconsolate on the bunk, curtains drawn, hungry and bored, trying his utmost to remember the words of the fifty-first Psalm: *'Have mercy on me, O God, according to your unfailing love; according to your great compassion blot out my transgressions. Wash away all my iniquity and cleanse me from my sin. For I know my transgressions, and my sin is always before me...'*

The words hummed in his head, making him sleepy. Beside him, the other two boys muttered and mumbled over their portions, and up and down the quarters other boys in other cabins sighed and suffered in the same way. They dared not play a game, or wrestle, or talk at all, or even doze, for at intervals the curtains were pulled apart and an adult came in to check their progress. The day seemed endless, with not even a share of the usual bean soup for dinner.

Towards evening there seemed to be a disturbance in another part of the quarters beyond the flimsy walls of their cabin. Voices, an exclamation, a woman's voice giving sharp orders. Then their blanket curtain was drawn quickly open. Tom sat upright, forming in his mind the words he would be asked to repeat. But it was Mistress Fuller, looking flushed and distracted. "Up on deck now, boys!"

"But we have been told to stay," protested Love. "We are not to move from here, my father said."

"Orders change when needs must," said Mistress Fuller briskly, giving them a push to hurry them on their way. "There's work to be done. Womens' work. Mistress Hopkins is come to her time."

The boys knew little of childbirth and were not greatly interested. They needed no second bidding to escape their imprisonment, clattering up to the deck with speed. Constance Hopkins and Elizabeth, the Tilleys' daughter, were heading for the ladder with pails of water and looks of importance on their faces. It was much colder, a chill wind thrummed through the rigging and strong winds sent spray over the decks. Tom shivered under his shirt and doublet and wondered if a storm was coming. Together they clung to the rails and watched the waves rear and crash against the bow of the *Mayflower*.

All of them were damp and shivering by the time Elizabeth Tilley appeared and told them that they could go below again. It seemed almost a relief to descend again into the steamy, smelly warmth. Tom hoped that they would be judged repentant enough to be given supper.

The curtains of the Hopkins' cabin were still tightly drawn, and from behind them came a strange thin crying like the mewling of a kitten.

"A boy," Elizabeth told them. "Strong and healthy. Born at sea, and so to be called Oceanus."

***

The autumn storms had come, and for days the ship tossed and pitched on angry seas that sprayed and soaked the decks with icy, drenching water. As the ship rolled, so the water seeped downward into the lower deck where the travellers were, so that the Pilgrims and Strangers, their clothes and bedding, were often damp and could not be properly dried out. Cooking on the braziers became impossible; meals now consisted of the hard ship's biscuit, dried salted meat and what remained of the cheese and butter brought from home, carefully eked out. Seasickness returned to some, and almost all developed coughs and colds from the chill and damp.

The travellers no longer went above; it was almost impossible to stand on the tilting and heaving deck. Day after day was spent huddled in their damp and musty bedding, with the coughing of the sick all around and the plaintive wailing of the newborn baby, while the timbers creaked and the waves lashed.

One day, a mighty crack sounded overhead and there were cries of alarm that sent the men scurrying to the ladders. A huge beam had broken, letting in even more water, and for a few minutes there was pandemonium. Some wanted to put about and head back for the shores of England. But then someone remembered something stowed away in the hold – a huge screw brought by the Separatists for lifting heavy timbers when they began the building of their homes. The screw was hauled up from below, with all hands working together, and manhandled into position to support the damaged beam. It held, and the *Mayflower* stayed on her set course.

Through it all, the Separatists, morning and evening, said their prayers and sang their praises to God. Nobody mocked them any longer. Instead, even the Strangers and the military men would listen respectfully, seeming to take comfort from these prayers. Tom would listen, his own fears subsiding as the Elders spoke to God as though he was there beside him in their troubles and hardships.

"Thou art the Master of the winds and waves," William Brewster prayed after one particularly rough and sleepless night. "We are helpless in our own strength, but thou art our refuge, and underneath us are thine everlasting arms. Our trust is in thee, that thou wilt carry us safe to land and bring about thy purposes for us."

Master Brewster prayed with his eyes open and his arms uplifted. And suddenly, Tom had the strong feeling that someone was there beside them in this stinking, storm-tossed, wet and heaving vessel, someone all-strong and all-powerful who could still the waves with a word if he so chose. Someone who knew each by name. He caught his breath. Someone who knew him, Tom Turner, and loved him greatly.

The feeling did not entirely leave, although the storm continued for many more days. Tom had lost count of how many days they had now been at sea. Fifty? Sixty?

The year must be coming towards winter. They had been warned by many about sailing so late in the year and maybe the warnings should have been heeded.

And then, suddenly, the seas grew calmer. William Bradford, the tall young man who was one of the leaders and a great friend of William Brewster, moved among the travellers, urging them to get up from their beds and stretch their cramped limbs. Tom and some of the others climbed the ladder, noticing that the lurching and shuddering had quietened. On deck, a cold wind blew but the worst of the storms had passed. One by one the travellers emerged and walked on deck, breathing fresh air for the first time in days.

At about mid-morning a cry arose from a lookout perched high in the rigging, a cry that set everyone searching the horizon.

"Land ho!"

Away to the west, a thin bluish line on the horizon showed them their first glimpse of the New World.

Chapter Eight

Tragedy

It was the ninth day of November, or so it was reckoned by those who had kept count of the days. They had been at sea for 65 days; more than two months.

But the trials, weariness, dangers, hunger and sickness seemed to fade into memory as they watched the distant continent grow slowly nearer. Tom stared at the land coming gradually into view, a long stretch of forest with trees still in their autumn colours of yellow and russet and scarlet, waves breaking on a strip of shore – their new home.

Nearby, the Pilgrim leaders were giving thanks. But there was a muttering among some of the Strangers.

"We were promised Virginia, and what's this place we're coming to? Somewhere different altogether," said Master Billington, father of John and Francis.

"Those storms blew us right off course," said another man. "We're well to the North. Cape Cod, that's what the Captain and crew are saying."

The ship drew closer to the rocky shores of Cape Cod, looking for a landing place. A lot of talk was going on, and not everyone seemed to be in agreement. The children listened, picking up bits here and there. In Virginia, there was land already waiting for them, good fertile land where already crops had been sown and gathered. There were settlements they'd been granted permission to join. They would be greeted and welcomed with roofs over their heads, and food and rest from their journey before beginning their own lives and work. Here, the land was wild and unsettled, no houses, maybe no people at all. Unless – the boys looked at each other and repeated the words with bated breath – unless there were Indians! The prospect filled them with a mixture of fear and excitement.

Landing was more difficult than they had expected. Slowly, Captain Jones edged the ship along the coastline, looking for a safe harbour, but it was not until two days later that they found a landing place. By then, they had made their way around the tip of the Cape and come into the sheltered bay beyond, where they were able at last to drop anchor.

Sailors climbed into the rigging to furl the sails, their purposes fulfilled. Master Brewster offered prayer and thanksgiving for a safe arrival. All of them gathered together on deck and were addressed by the Captain and all the leaders.

"We need to agree formally that we will support and assist one another and abide by rules laid down for the good of us all," said William Bradford, and there was a chorus of agreement. The rules were drawn up there and then and duly signed by all the adult men in the party, Separatists and Strangers alike. By common consent, a well-respected older man called John Carver was elected their first Governor.

Tom gazed across the bay at the new land, mysterious and unknown, a tangled mass of tall trees and vegetation. Did unseen eyes look out at them from the shelter of the forest? Meanwhile, an advance party was making ready to row to the shore. The shallop, a small boat designed for use in shallower water, had suffered some damage on the voyage and was in need of repair. The sound of hammering echoed around the ship while impatience grew. At last it was ready and launched, with the first party to set foot on land for many days. William Bradford took his place among them, after a tearful farewell from his wife Dorothy. The others lined the ship's rails as the boat began its journey to land. What would be discovered there?

"How soon can we all go?" demanded Love Brewster, watching the boat depart and dancing from one foot to another with impatience. "I'm tired of this ship! I want to see some Indians!"

"Hush, foolish boy!" his mother said sternly. "You may have many more days to wait yet. This may not be our final resting place. We need to practise much patience while we see how the land lies."

She made the boys shake out the damp, musty bedding and air it on deck. The men had promised that the women should soon go ashore to find fresh water and wash clothes, a much-needed task after so many days at sea.

And there were still many sick among the passengers, and many weak, thin and feeble. William Button, the young servant of Samuel Fuller, had died not long before landfall, and there had been another burial at sea. But renewed hope brought its own courage.

Later a fresh storm blew up, and it was feared that the shallop would receive more battering before it reached the shore. As night fell, the ship rocked at anchor and there was more activity below decks – another baby was born, a son, Peregrine, to Susanna and William White, a baby brother for 5-year-old Resolved. The travellers wrapped themselves in their blankets and settled to sleep.

It had been a long and exhausting day and the travellers' quarters were soon silent except for the snorings and mutterings of sleepers. Tom had been deeply asleep but woke suddenly to a muffled thump from above. Someone had left a hatch unbattened, he guessed. It came again, and he wondered why no one went to fasten it. He guessed the crew were exhausted too. He was drifting off to sleep again when another thump came. There was nothing for it. He had no idea how far from morning they were; this banging could go on for hours. Nobody else was awake, so he'd have to go up and close it himself. He thought of waking Love or Richard and asking them to go with him, and gave Richard's arm a nudge. Richard snorted and turned over in his sleep, digging Love in the ribs and causing the younger boy to mutter and yank the blankets closer around himself. Neither was going to be pleased to be awoken from their slumber. Tom sighed. It would be less trouble to go alone.

The hatch to their quarters was open, shifting slightly with the swell and causing the bumping. The worst of the storm had passed; above the deck, stars shone from an ink-black sky and the moon was half-full, with a skein of dark cloud scudding across its surface. Tom hesitated. He'd never been above decks after dark before and the night sky looked beautiful. After a moment, he pulled himself up onto the deck.

The night air was chill, and he shivered a little. There wasn't much to see after all, clouds were blotting out the moonlight again and the water lapped dark as ink below the rails. A keen wind whipped through his thin shirt, and Tom turned back to the companionway. Then another sound came to his ears above the lap of the waves – the sound of a woman's weeping.

Tom had heard that sound before, that soft, despairing, breathless sobbing. He'd heard it when

William Bradford climbed aboard the shallop that morning, and once before when he'd come across William's wife Dorothy weeping in a quiet corner of the deck when she'd thought she was alone. And then he could see her – a dark, slight shape at the rail beyond the rigging, clinging to the rail and crying almost silently, but with a desolation that pierced him to the heart.

All in a moment, Tom remembered his mother weeping in just the same way, when she fancied herself alone, pouring out her bitter heartbreak where none would know. He could do nothing for his mother, but maybe he could offer some comfort to Dorothy Bradford. Silently, on bare feet, he began to make his way through the rigging to where she stood.

Suddenly the clouds parted and he saw her clearly for a moment, a small thin figure in her night-shift, her face lifted to gaze across the ocean, back in the direction of the Old World, where her son was. Then the scudding clouds cut off the view, and in the sudden darkness Tom's bare toe collided painfully with a metal ring holding a rope. He gasped and clutched his toe for a moment, until the pain eased a little. Suddenly his head jerked up. A sudden splash had come from somewhere ahead of him, and when he looked again at where Dorothy had stood, there was nobody at the rail.

When Tom half-tumbled below into the travellers' quarters to raise the alarm, there was immediate activity.

Travellers and seamen alike swarmed on deck, scanning the dark waves for the shape of a small woman. Nothing could be seen in the darkness, although in fact the sky was already lightening and dawn was coming. It was not until an hour or more later that Dorothy's body was found, floating face-down in the cold waters of Cape Cod bay.

Instead of the joy and excitement that should have greeted the returning explorers, there was instead a heavy weight of grief and sadness. William Bradford, stricken at the loss of his wife, was silent and withdrawn. It was whispered that he reproached himself bitterly for bringing his pretty young wife on the voyage and separating her from their 5-year-old son left behind in Holland. She had felt the parting keenly, everyone knew that. There were some who were not surprised that her sadness was so great that she had ended her own life. Others felt she may have fallen overboard by accident.

"Do you think I might have saved her?" asked Tom tearfully on that sad morning. But Mary Brewster would have none of that, and put a comforting arm around him and said that there were times when what would be, would be.

And life for the rest must go on. The exploring party told of what they had found. The men were exhausted and had worsened coughs and colds from sleeping out in the open without shelter. Soon after landing, they had caught sight of brown-skinned bodies amongst the trees, who seemed to melt away at their approach. They had made camp on the beach, lit a fire and taken off their soaked outer garments, hanging them on bushes to dry. During the night, strange cries had come from deep in the forest, something like the howling of wild dogs or wolves. They had slept only fitfully and towards dawn were jerked awake by a hail of arrows from the sheltering trees. By the mercy of God, said William Bradford, none had hit the men, but their drying clothes had been shot through with arrows. Maybe the garments had been mistaken for the men themselves.

Miles Standish had seized his musket, already primed and loaded, and fired it off. The others followed suit. Their attackers fled, disappearing silently into the trees. But the newcomers were aware of unseen eyes watching as they continued their exploration, pushing through the trees that fringed the coastline in search of a place where houses could be built and land cultivated.

They had not been successful. Fresh water would be needed and none could be found. Nor was there the kind of land that could be cleared and made ready for crops. The forest grew thick and dense all about and the ground was full of roots and undergrowth. Winter was fast approaching and shelter would be needed against the cold. The native Indians had proved themselves hostile.

They must return to the ship and travel further along the coastline to find a safe haven.

Returning towards the bay, the men had discovered strange mounds under the earth. Investigation found that they contained buried stores of corn. There must have been ground fit for cultivation not too far away. Were these stores the property of the Indians? Or had white settlers travelled this way before? Soon afterwards, half buried in the sand, they came across a large tin kettle, also filled with corn. Maybe there had been traders visiting these waters too.

Stores on the *Mayflower* were getting dangerously low. Would it be permissible to take some of the corn for themselves? Any objections were overruled. They took the kettle and carried it back to the shallop, adding to it whatever fruits and berries from the trees that were ripe and judged to be edible. The families back on board had tasted no fresh food for many weeks, and scurvy was an ever-present danger.

They had little good news to offer, but this was better than nothing. They climbed into the shallop and pushed off, never guessing that the saddest news of all awaited them back on the *Mayflower*.

Chapter Nine

The forest

The untimely death of Dorothy Bradford cast a gloom over the travellers on the *Mayflower*, adding to their trials of sickness, hunger, weakness and discouragement. It was getting colder too. As the month wore on they could not help but be aware that winter had come, and that the winters here would be cold and harsh.

And still they had not found their settling place. Patiently, they tried to pray and hope and trust, while parties of men went out in the shallop to explore the coastline in search of a suitable place to build their homes. Sometimes some of the women were taken in the boat to the shore, to do the washing of clothes which was so badly needed. And one never-to-be-forgotten afternoon, some of the bigger boys went too.

"There are still berries and fruits in the woods," said Mistress Mullins, returning from one of the laundry visits, her hands red and raw from the cold water. "Some of you lads could busy yourselves and gather some for us. We sorely need fresh food."

Some of the passengers were showing symptoms which Samuel Fuller's father, who had some medical knowledge, said were the first signs of scurvy: aching muscles and a loosening of the teeth. Fresh fruit would be a vital addition to their diet. So the next day, a group of the bigger boys, Joseph, Richard, Francis, John, Samuel and Tom, were rowed to land with willow baskets and instructed to forage.

"Don't waste time in idle play," they were admonished by their elders. "And don't pick poisonous berries. The boat will come and fetch you back before dusk."

Tom found himself standing on the beach, with the thick tangle of forest to one side and the expanse of grey water with the *Mayflower* riding at anchor on the other. The forest birches, oaks and maples had few leaves left clinging to their branches now and stood bare and stark among thick undergrowth. The land itself felt strange under his feet, no rocking motion and creak of the ship's timbers, just firm sand under his boots and the wind rattling the bare twigs and ruffling the surface of the waves.

The boys looked at each other. "Well, let's go to it," said Samuel.

"Do you think there might be Indians in the woods?" asked Richard.

It was a sobering thought that eyes might be watching from behind tree trunks, arrows strung to bows. Even John Billington seemed a little less sure of himself now that they were on their own. All too fresh in their minds was the experience the men had had at their first landing place. And they had all heard plenty of tales of white children being taken captive by Indians. Tom felt himself shiver a little in the chilly wind. He felt more frightened than he cared to admit. Suddenly the *Mayflower* and its cramped, smelly quarters seemed the safest place on earth to be.

"Let's go," said Samuel again.

Nobody would admit to being too scared to enter the forest. Clutching their baskets, they set off into the woods. Many paths criss-crossed between the trees, worn by bear and deer, small animals and maybe human feet too. Fallen leaves made a thick mould underfoot, and it was dim and silent between tall trees, bare now of most of their summer foliage. But on the undergrowth and bushes berries still clung – blackberries, rose hips, haws and some that they did not recognise at all. The boys began to gather them, trying to put some into the baskets as well as their mouths.

It was a slow and laborious task though. "This is girls' work," said Francis disgustedly after half an hour of picking. "They should have sent the girls over to do this."

"They'd have been too scared to come into the forest," said Samuel. He mimicked a girl's high voice. "Mercy upon us, I think there's a snake! Help, I see a most fearsome spider! Oh, oh, is that an Indian creeping up upon us!"

They laughed, though a little uneasily at the mention of Indians. But nobody wanted to be compared to a bunch of girls. "I think we should spread out," said Samuel. "We're all going after the same few berries. We'd get a lot more if we all picked separately. Let's each take a path to ourselves. It'll be easy to follow the paths back the way we came."

Tom felt a lurch of terror at the thought of being cut off from the others in this strange, dim forest. Already the grey of the bay water could only be seen in glimpses between the tall trunks. But again nobody would admit to being afraid. And so it was that he found himself alone on one of the little pathways leading deeper into the tangled woodland.

The boys called to one another, to reassure themselves as much as anything. The voices were growing fainter and more muffled. Tom's eyes darted about, looking for the shiny scarlet of rose hips or the dark gloss of blackberries. There were other berries too, small and dark in bunches, and something yellowish that he thought was a plum but could not be sure. There were small sour crab apples and wild pears. Much of the fruit had been pecked by birds or nibbled by insects or had fallen and begun to rot, but there was still much to be had. His basket began to look less empty.

And then suddenly he realised that he hadn't heard any of the other boys' voices for some while. He straightened up and listened. Apart from the odd creaks and rustlings of the forest, there was an eerie silence. He called out, his voice sounding a little wavering, "Joseph? John? Samuel! Hallooo! Can you hear me?"

No answer, except for a startled squawk and a clatter of wings from a bird he had alarmed. Tom looked about him. Now he could no longer see the bay at all. He had turned aside more than once at sight of some new bramble patch and now was not sure which was the first pathway he had taken. They all looked the same, twining away into deeper woodland. He was not even sure of the direction of the bay.

He was lost. The realisation came as he called again, this time more urgently. Still no answer. His heart thumped hard and he felt sick. Would they search for him? Surely he would not be left alone here! What if darkness fell before they came? He tried to quell the rising panic inside. What would William Brewster tell him to do?

He would tell you to trust God.

The thought came like a ray of light. That is what he must do. But how? And would God bother to help him? Or was he not important enough to bother with?

Suddenly, he was aware that he was not alone. From out of the trees a figure had come and was standing quite silently in front of him on the pathway. It was a boy, but not one of the *Mayflower* boys. This boy was slightly smaller than himself, maybe about the age of Love Brewster. Despite the cold, he wore only leggings of some skin and a waistcoat of the same skin. His bare feet were thrust into moccasins, his hair coarse and black, tied around with a leather thong. His skin was a coppery brown, his eyes bright and dark.

Tom knew at once that he was an Indian. Strangely, he felt no fear, just a strong sense of relief. The two of them stared at each other for a long moment. Then the boy said something in a strange language, pointing at the basket in Tom's hand. He motioned towards the deeper forest with one brown hand. Tom noticed a leather pouch and a sheath with a knife handle at his waist. He hesitated and then said, "I'm lost. I want to find my friends."

The boy looked at him. Tom felt he had not understood because he only beckoned to Tom to follow. Tom had a flicker of doubt, but only for a moment. Somehow he knew that no harm was meant by this small boy. He followed.

The Indian boy led the way to where the trees thinned into a kind of clearing. There, bushes grew thickly, covered with small purplish berries that were unfamiliar to Tom. The boy pointed to the berries and then to Tom's basket. Tom hesitated again. He did not know whether these berries were safe to eat, or poisonous, or anything about them. The boy seemed to sense the reason for his hesitation. He picked a handful of the berries himself and stuffed them into his own mouth, chewing them with every sign of great enjoyment, then held some out to Tom. Tom found them sweet but with a delicious sharpness that made him want more. He found himself picking another handful and eating them. For a few moments they both gorged themselves on the berries until their mouths were stained purple. Somehow they filled a need in Tom that he hadn't realised he had.

After a moment, the Indian boy began to place handfuls of berries into Tom's basket. Tom had almost forgotten his reason for being here, and the fact that the others were nowhere to be found. He must try again to trace them, but he thought he might as well have something to show for himself when he did. The coming of the Indian boy had strangely relieved his fears. He set about picking with a will.

After a while they both straightened up, the basket almost full. Tom thought that it was a little darker, the short winter day beginning to draw to a close.

"I must get back," he said and pointed in the direction he thought the bay must be.

The Indian boy's keen dark eyes stared into his for a moment, and then understanding seemed to dawn. He nodded and set off along a path, motioning Tom to follow. It was not the direction Tom would have chosen, and he had a moment's doubt. But after a short time of following the winding pathways, the trees began to thin. Another few yards and the glimmer of water shone between them and, a moment later, boys' and men's voices sounded from the beach, voices he recognised.

The boy stopped, looked at him for a moment and then turned and disappeared without another word, silent as a shadow between the trees. Tom wanted to ask him to wait, to thank him for his help, but the boy was gone as suddenly as he had come.

There was relief when he emerged from the forest, mixed with annoyance, because the boat had come to fetch the boys and found one missing. The sailors had been debating whether to begin searching or whether it would be a waste of time.

Their annoyance was eased a little by the sight of Tom's full basket of fruit and berries. The other boys were envious. Their own efforts had gained more meagre pickings.

"How did you get such a lot all by yourself?" asked Richard.

Tom didn't reply at once. Then he said, "I wasn't by myself. Somebody came and helped me. An - an Indian boy."

They were heading across the beach to the waiting boat. Several stopped in their tracks and Tom saw amazement on all their faces. Disbelief, too, on some.

"I don't believe you," said John Billington flatly. "We never saw any Indians. And they wouldn't have helped you pick berries! Scalped you, more like!" He gave a short laugh, and some of the others laughed too, a little uneasily.

"You're jesting, aren't you, Tom?" said Samuel uncertainly.

Tom shook his head. "There was one. A boy. I lost my way and he showed me, after we'd picked the berries."

But already the encounter seemed strangely dreamlike.

"I reckon you fell asleep and dreamed it," observed Francis shrewdly.

"Then who picked the berries?" asked Joseph.

The men were calling them to get into the boat, as it would soon be night and they wanted to be back on board. Tom was aware of the sideways glances of the other boys as they climbed in. They were not prepared to believe his story. A lump of misery began to settle in his stomach, but Joseph nudged him with his elbow as they settled in the rocking boat and whispered, "Pay no heed, Tom. They're only envious because you got to see an Indian and they didn't!" Tom was comforted, although the other boys could not let the matter lie and alternately questioned him and ridiculed him all the way back to the *Mayflower*.

"You'd be lying back there in the woods with your scalp dangling off someone's belt if you'd really seen an Indian!" said John Billington scornfully as they reached the ship and prepared to scramble aboard. "You're scared to death of them, you know you are, Tom Turner!"

Tom didn't reply, but inside he thought wonderingly, I was, but I'm not now. Not any more.

If Tom's story was a strange one, the tale brought back by the returning explorers was stranger still. They had travelled a little further north and had made an overnight camp on the shore. During the night, some tools left at the edge of the camp had disappeared. Next day, Peter Browne caught a glimpse of an Indian, standing and watching from the brow of a hill among the trees. They guessed a village might be nearby, and maybe if they approached unarmed they would be able to make friendly contact. Some of the party were dubious about this plan, but William Bradford prevailed. Surely, he reasoned, it would be better to establish peaceful relations than making enemies of the people here before them, who knew and understood the land, how to grow crops and how to survive. Better to make friends with them if it could be done.

Early next morning the party had set out, leaving the shoreline and plunging deeper into the thick forest. The night before, they'd heard strange noises, screechings, howlings and hooting, and were not at all sure what kinds of animals might live there. Deeper and deeper they pressed forward through tangled brambles and undergrowth, until suddenly the path widened and they could see in front of them a clearing where huts with thatched roofs stood huddled together. They had reached an Indian village.

They paused, each man doing what came most instinctively to him. Miles Standish fingered his musket, and the hands of some of the others went to their weapons too. William Bradford offered a silent prayer and strode ahead into the clearing, holding his hands high to show that he came in peace. There was no answer to his greeting. Suddenly all of them noticed that the village was silent, no smoke rose from the dwellings and the only movement was from some tattered skin coverings on the buildings flapping in the wind. The whole place seemed deserted.

The men stepped forward cautiously. Could this be some kind of trap, an ambush? But as they approached the nearest dwelling, a terrifying sight met their eyes. Near the doorway were the ashes and remains of a fire, blown about and scattered by the wind, and beside them a large pot obviously used for cooking. The pot had been overturned and lay on its side. Nearby lay what had once been a human being but was now little more than a skeleton, probably a woman, because a much smaller skeleton lay close beside it. Shocked, the men's eyes darted round the clearing and saw other bones – a skull showing near the door flap of a hut, a skeleton huddled with drawn-up knees under a hawthorn tree, another lying full-length beside a half-built dug-out canoe. There were men, women and children. Scraps of blanket and animal skins clung to some of the bones, some had arrows in quivers and bows lying near to them. Some of the bones had been gnawed and scattered by scavenging animals. Not a living soul was anywhere in the village.

The men removed their hats and stood in stunned silence, even those among them who were hardened soldiers. At last William Bradford cleared his throat and said, "A whole village wiped out. It seems they just fell and died wherever they happened to be. What could cause this?"

"No sign of violence," said Standish. "And it happened very suddenly. Some kind of sickness?"

"Plague?" asked Bradford. But no one had any answer. Whatever had destroyed the people of the village, it had come and gone, leaving none to tell the tale.

The men had no further heart for exploration that day. Pondering on what they'd seen, they made their way back to make their report to the rest of the company.

***

*L*ater, the *Mayflower* pilgrims were to learn that other communities of Indians had also died suddenly and mysteriously, of a malady that came without warning and struck them where they stood. It was believed that a sickness had been brought by some trading ship and spread rapidly among people who had no defences against it.

All on the *Mayflower* were shocked by the discovery of the stricken village. But soon after this news came other, more hopeful tidings. At last a promising settling place had been discovered, and they would be making their final landfall there.

Chapter Ten

New world

They called the new place Plymouth, after the English town they had set sail from all those weeks ago, where the townspeople had been very kind to them as they waited. The new place seemed to offer in abundance everything they could wish for. There was a safe harbour, two streams of fresh water and land that could be cultivated for crops. Pine, oak, birch, hemlock and hickory grew in plenty for the building of houses and farm buildings, furniture and tool handles, and a profusion of game and fish roamed the forest and swam in the waters.

If only it had been summer time, and the people fit and well! As it was, mid-December had come before the *Mayflower* dropped its anchors in the bay, and it had rained most of the time for several weeks. The travellers were weak from poor rations and lack of fresh food, and sick with coughs and colds that would not get better.

Nevertheless, the strongest and fittest men took their tools, went ashore and began at once the work of felling trees and constructing the first buildings. Until shelter was ready, most of the Pilgrims and Strangers would have to stay on the ship. But nobody missed the opportunity to get to land whenever there was room on the shallop or the rowing boat.

Tom, with a couple of the other boys, was offered the chance to go ashore one day when, for once, it was not raining, though a cold wind whipped the water into whitecaps and the skies were grey and lowering.

"Snow about," grunted the Billington boys' father, who was one of the working party for that day.

John Alden was there too, always cheerful, though his face had grown thinner over the weeks at sea. He was chatting to Priscilla Mullins who, with some of the other girls and women, had brought a load of washing to do in the freshwater stream.

Francis Billington nudged Tom. "He's sweet on her!"

Tom looked across and saw that Priscilla's usually pale cheeks had a tinge of pink as she clutched her cloak about her and listened to the young cooper explaining how the first building was being constructed. It was to be a large square building of split pine logs, at the very top of the hill, and would serve as a fort and lookout post as well as temporary housing while the separate homes were being built. From there, the other houses would straggle downhill towards the shore, on either side of a village 'street'. Each would have its own fenced garden patch and enclosures for pigs and hens and goats, when they could be procured. In time, they'd even have a cow or two, for milk and cheese and butter. The men would clear more land for corn crops, and the women would tend their own vegetable patches and their own homes. And on the Lord's day, all would meet together at the big house for worship and praise, with no fear of punishment for breaking the king's rules.

"It sounds like heaven itself," said Priscilla wistfully. "If only it could happen as you say."

"We will make it happen," said John Alden staunchly.

They had reached the shore, and Tom noticed how carefully John helped Priscilla to step ashore, first taking the bundle of washing from her. It's true, he is sweet on her, he thought, a little embarrassed. But, at the same time, he had a sudden bittersweet memory of himself as a small boy, watching his father help his mother to cross a wintry patch of ice and snow. It seemed now like another time, another life. Yet he felt tears fill his eyes at the thought, though he brushed them away and pretended they were just because of the bitter wind.

Mistress Carver was handing him a wooden pail, and another to Francis and Samuel. "Look out for mussels and shellfish along the shore. But choose carefully, only those that are fresh. Remember that those we ate at Cape Cod made us very sick."

Picking mussels from cold rocks with freezing hands was not the most appealing of pastimes, but all of them were learning that cold hands were better than empty bellies. The grey water lapped at their feet, while above on the hill there was sawing and hammering as the building work went on. A little way along the shore, where fresh water emptied into salt, the women and girls were scrubbing clothes on the rocks and rinsing them in the cold water, a chillier task even than mussel picking.

The boys had each brought a piece of ship's biscuit and salt pork to eat at noon. And after these were eaten Francis Billington declared that he would work no longer.

"I'm going up the hill," he said. "Maybe I can get a rabbit with my catapult."

The others needed little persuasion, though Tom thought that no rabbit would be showing itself with all that hammering and banging going on. They climbed the muddy slope to the top of the hill. Some of the timber framework was already in place, the raw new wood standing out in contrast to the weathered trunks of the forest trees. Despite the cold, the men were sweating as they toiled. Some were coughing and had to stop often to catch their breath. Progress seemed painfully slow. Around them the forest brooded dark and mysterious, the leaves now gone from the trees. Tom thought of the Indian village with none left alive in it, and shivered. That morning, a baby had been born dead on board the *Mayflower*. It seemed like another bad omen, though Elder Brewster had said talk of omens was the devil's work and that it was in God they all must place their trust.

Already it was beginning to grow dark, the short winter day closing in. Down on the beach the women had lit a small fire and had rigged up a makeshift washing line between two tree saplings. They would spread out the washing and leave it there overnight and, provided it did not rain again, the heat of the fire while it lasted might begin to dry the clothes.

John Alden greeted the boys cheerfully and asked them to fetch him a drink of water from the stream. He looked at the lowering sky as he drank. A few snowflakes were falling. Tom shivered again suddenly, cold and tired and hungry and weary of all those things. John looked at his downcast face and said with a smile, "Cheer up, Tom Turner. You know what the day after tomorrow is? It's Christmas Day!"

***

If the children had expected any Christmas celebrations, they were sadly disappointed. Christmas Eve had fallen on a Sunday, and of course there was no work that day, not even the cooking of food. Instead, they gathered on the shore to sing psalms and to pray, and to listen to a sermon by William Brewster which seemed to Tom to be even longer than usual. He took as his text a verse from the book of Ephesians: *Giving thanks always for all things unto God and the Father in the name of our Lord Jesus Christ.* He said they should have thankful hearts, especially to the Father for the gift of his only Son for the redemption of a sinful world.

The Pilgrims listened, shivering, wrapped in their cloaks and seated on fallen branches from the forest's edge. The spoken words were often punctuated by coughings and splutterings from the congregation, and most of the listening faces were pinched and white. Even the children had little energy to fidget but huddled close to their parents for warmth and comfort, wishing the homily was over. Tom sat between the two Brewster boys, wishing there was a hot dinner to look forward to when the meeting was over, wishing there were soles to repair his boots, which were beginning to let in the wet, wishing his hands weren't chapped red and raw, wishing...

***

*B*ut his wishes had carried him too far, back to a world with a warm fire and food and Christmas celebrations, and a mother and father and Sarah and Ellen and John and the littlest baby... And suddenly there were tears on his cheeks and he had to clench his fists hard and drag himself back into the present.

Mistress Brewster seemed to notice and understand; she reached across little Wrestling and gave his hand a quick squeeze, and he was grateful for her kindness.

Next day, no Christmas cheer awaited the *Mayflower* Pilgrims. There would be no roast goose, no sweetmeats, no merrymaking or gifts or telling of stories around a blazing hearth, no families celebrating the birth of the Christ Child. The Separatist leaders declared that there was no need of man-made ritual and feast days; God should be honoured every day by obedience to his Word. Instead, Governor Carver declared that it would be a working day like any other. It was not the Sabbath, and work must go forward if they were to be housed against the worst of the winter to come. Already a light powdering of snow covered the highest ground. Some of the Strangers looked askance at this harsh decision and there were mutterings from members of the crew. A few of them refused point blank to join the work party and rowed a barrel of beer over to the shore. There they lit a fire and sat drinking until they grew merry, when their singing and laughter could be heard from the decks of the *Mayflower* at anchor in the bay.

"Shame on them, and may they be served right, with sore heads in the morning," said Mistress Chilton, who had come on deck with Mistress Mullins to empty buckets from the quarters below.

"No, no, pray for their souls," said Mistress Mullins. "Remember, none of us is without a weakness."

"And some more than most," said Mistress Chilton, and would have said more if at that moment Mistress Carver had not called up from below asking for fresh water and cloths, because both Remember Allerton and Giles Hopkins had gone down with sudden fevers.

Chapter Eleven

The sickness

Now began the worst time of all for the travellers on the *Mayflower* – Separatists, Strangers and crew alike. Sickness spread like wildfire, a sudden raging fever that brought with it aching limbs and often delirium, leaving the sufferer weak and with a hacking cough, if they recovered at all.

Many did not recover. Three days after her baby's stillbirth, Mary Allerton was laid to rest beside it in the place on the hilltop that came to be named Burial Hill. A little while afterwards, Richard More's small brother and sister, lodged with other families, died of the sickness and were buried in small graves, leaving Richard white and silent, with no family now but the Brewsters, who comforted him as best they could. In every family someone was sick. Both Elizabeth Tilley's parents were laid low, as was brisk Mistress Chilton and her husband. Captain Standish's sweet wife Rose was struck down with the terrible fever and died in a few days. A few days later William White died also, leaving his wife Susanna with 5-year-old Resolved and the new baby Peregrine, born at Cape Cod. As the days of the New Year passed slowly, so the ship became daily more like a hospital; sometimes it seemed that there were more sick than well people left to tend them.

But through it all, the strongest and fittest continued with the work of building the common-house and clearing ground for the sowing of some winter crops. One day, Governor Carver asked the older children to help with the building by collecting thick clay from the stream beds to chink between the boards in the big house and make it watertight and windproof.

"This is worse than picking shrimps and mussels," said Francis Billington in disgust, slapping handfuls of cold wet clay into a bucket.

"Be thankful that you are still able to be useful," said Elizabeth Tilley sharply, "or that you're alive at all."

Only four days before, Elizabeth had watched with tears streaming down her cheeks as the body of her father was loaded into the boat to be taken for burial. There had been no time to grieve; even the girls now had to help with the labour of building.

By the time they carried the last bucket of clay to the new common-house, Tom ached from head to foot. The building was almost complete and was being thatched, and already several smaller buildings were being constructed along the village street.

Tom was tired to the bone, chilled, plastered with mud. His boots had let in the wet, his head ached and his throat was sore. He felt Governor Carver's hand on his shoulder. "You worked hard today, Tom. Well done."

The words cheered Tom's heart as the workers stumbled wearily down the hill towards the waiting boat. But once on board, he began to shiver uncontrollably, aching in every joint and limb. By the time they were on board again, he had to be half-carried up the ladder and taken below to his pallet. He could not touch the hot broth offered him by Mistress Hopkins, and was soon burning with fever.

For a long time Tom knew little, alternately burning and shivering, aching in every part of his body. Sometimes he felt he was back in his childhood home, with the sun shining in through the open door and his sisters playing cat's cradle on the doorstep. He wanted to tell them something, warn them of some danger that threatened, but no words would come from his dry throat and cracked lips.

And then, suddenly, everything was right again, because his mother was there, putting a damp cloth to his hot brow and speaking soothing words. "There, Tom, there. You'll be better now, thanks be to God."

He saw that it was not his mother but Mary Brewster, thin and pale herself but with a smile in her blue eyes. All around him were the smells of sickness and sounds of groans and coughing. He felt a moment's keen regret.

It would have been so easy to slip away, to let go of life and find peace in another place...

But Mistress Brewster was holding a basin and spooning warm liquid into his mouth. He drank it down and, despite himself, felt strength return.

"Three days you've been sick, Tom," she said. "But it's pleased God to answer our prayers and spare you."

Others had not been so fortunate. Over the last few days, no less than seven people had lost their battle with the sickness. The father and mother of Priscilla Mullins lay mortally sick and little hope was held for their recovery, and their son Joseph had gone down with fever too.

Tom sat up. His head was swimming and his limbs felt weak and heavy, but the fever was gone. He coughed a little but already sensed that it was not the deep, racking cough that afflicted so many of the others, but something that would soon ease. He struggled to rise, but Mistress Brewster pushed him back. "Rest a bit, Tom. Then maybe you can help tend some of the others."

She told him that some of the sick had been rowed over to land and lodged in the new common-house, away from the stench and disease of the ship. A great fire burned there, indeed, so well it burned that a spark had flown up into the thatch and almost set the whole place ablaze. Governor Carver and William Bradford had both been there that day, but thanks be to God they and everyone else had been saved and the fire put out.

"Are they sick too then?" asked Tom, thinking of the strong leaders.

Mary Brewster nodded. "More have been sick than have not. We have been hard pressed to care for them all, and have not been able to save the worst afflicted. Almost every night there has been a burial, or more than one."

"At night?"

"Yes." She paused for a moment and went on, "More Indians have been seen, up on the hill, watching our work go on. We don't know what they might do. But it is best that they do not know how many of our number have died, how much our company is weakened. So our men bury the dead at night, up on the hill where the corn is to be planted, and make the ground flat so none can tell. They will plant corn over them."

Tears stood in her kind eyes. Later that year, God willing, green spikes of corn would push up over the graves of the Pilgrims, and later still, long tassels and full kernels to be harvested against the winter. And among those quiet dead would lie whole families, mothers, fathers and children who had so bravely set sail upon the *Mayflower*.

She brushed away a tear and rose to her feet. "Now, if I help you, maybe you can stand on your feet. There is much to do, both here and on the land. Some of the crew have the sickness too. When the next boat comes in, you shall go across to join the others in the big house."

In another few days, Tom was in the big common-house, which still smelt of fresh-sawn timber and which was to be fort and look-out point above and meeting room below, but which at present seemed more like a hospital. He was still weak himself, but growing stronger by the day. Game was plentiful in the winter woods, and some days there was rabbit, duck, or even venison to provide meat for the workers and nourishing broth for the sick. The work went on whenever there were men fit to do it, but sometimes all that could be done was tend to the sick. A fortunate few did not get the sickness at all, among them Captain Miles Standish and William Brewster. These two took their fair share of caring for the sick: cooking, feeding, washing and tending them as carefully as any woman. Tom and the other surviving children helped, holding a cup to a thirsty mouth, fetching water, collecting wood for the fire, doing whatever was needful.

In the month of February there were more deaths and more secret burials under cover of the night. In the second week Priscilla Mullins' mother and father died, and shortly afterwards her brother Joseph, Tom's playmate and friend.

On the morning after Joseph's burial, Tom went to fetch water from the stream, but instead felt a great wave of grief well up inside him. He sat on a fallen log beside the water and buried his head in his hands, remembering Joseph laughing and running on the beach, daring him to climb the rigging, sitting on a coil of rope on the deck and wondering what adventures they would find in the New World. Now it would never happen, for Joseph and so many others. This New World was a hard, cold, hungry and cruel place to be, even for those who lived. He had heard talk lately that many were saying, if they lived they would return to England when the *Mayflower* sailed. This place was too full of grief and suffering, more than they could bear. For the first time, Tom felt that he would go back too, if the chance was offered.

There was a hand on his shoulder and William Brewster was there, sitting creakily down beside him. The Elder had aged a great deal over the past hard months; he looked grey and shrunken and weary beyond belief. But the kindness was still there in his grey eyes.

"Is it Joseph you grieve for?" he asked gently.

Tom nodded, and felt the hot tears trickle through his fingers.

Elder Brewster was silent for a moment. Then he sighed deeply. "I grieve too, for these young ones, their lives so quickly spent. Sometimes I question the wisdom of the pathway we took to secure our freedom. But then—" He paused, and looked at the muddy, trampled village street, at the half-completed buildings and piles of sawn timber, at the leafless trees and grey skies. He sighed again, and went on, "Then remember God's thoughts are not our thoughts and his ways not our ways, but that he is above all a God of love."

Tom felt a big sob rise to the surface. He burst out, "How can he be when you pray for all these and still they die..."

He stopped suddenly, shocked at his own daring. Never before had he spoken so disrespectfully to one of the Pilgrims, let alone showed his doubts about their God.

But William Brewster pressed his shoulder gently. "Why some die and some live I cannot answer. Our lives are in God's hands, and the span of them his to decide. But this I know - when we weep, he weeps also. He knows our sorrows. Did he not freely give his own Son as a sacrifice for our sins? Because we are his, it does not mean that we will not know pain and loss and suffer heartbreak in this life. His Son himself promised that we would have all these things. But he also promised that he would be with us in all our trials, would never leave us and in the end would guide us safely home. And all these now lost to us have already reached that home."

Tom was silent. Despite himself, he felt a comfort in these words. And just that morning he had heard one of the *Mayflower* crewmen remark that the Pilgrims truly cared for the sick and made no difference between Separatists, Strangers and seamen, while the crew thought only of themselves and their own needs. Certainly William Brewster and his family and the other Pilgrims had shown Tom as much love as if he were their own. Were they truly good people by their nature, or was it their God who made the difference?

William Brewster was rising stiffly to his feet. "Come, Tom, they need that water for breakfast porridge. Let us get back to the fire, and eat, and be about our work for today. We will not forget those gone from us, but there are many still living to care for."

Chapter Twelve

Indian visitors

Tom stepped outside the Brewster cabin and at once felt something different in the air. It was still cold, but there was a softness in the air he hadn't felt for many months. Off in the woods a bird warbled, and another answered it. When he looked closely, he could see the very first beginnings of tiny green buds appearing on the hawthorns and that the hazels and willows had powdery yellow catkins swinging from their twigs. It was the middle of March, and spring was on its way.

Swinging the water buckets, Tom climbed to the deep clear pool in the stream where it was easy to dip up water. The settlers had already christened the stream the Town Brook, as it was the source of most of their fresh water. He saw that the mosses here looked fresh and green, and that new grass was sprouting all along the stream banks. He filled the buckets and put them down for a moment, looking down over the village.

A few temporary huts of wattle and daub had been built to provide immediate shelter over the winter, but already several more substantial houses of sawn timber and thatch straggled down the hill towards the sweep of blue-grey sea beyond. Some were still half-built; others, like the Brewster home, complete enough for the family to have moved in. Almost everyone had moved from the ship into the village now; those still single and children orphaned by the sickness had been taken in by one or other of the families. Two of the hens which had belonged to Mistress Chilton were brooding eggs and the children awaited the first hatching with excitement. The two dogs, mastiff and spaniel, daily sniffed new and tantalising scents from the woods, and often brought home a rabbit or a game bird for the pot.

But, despite these hopeful signs of new life and new beginnings, the memory of that terrible winter was still fresh in the minds of them all. Who could soon forget the hunger, the sickness, the harsh weather, the cruel disappointments, the cold and the wet and unrelenting hard toil? Half of the colony had died before they had a chance to settle. Many of those who lived were still weak, most mourned the death of loved ones, a few had been injured in accidents, all were thin and pale and their faces told of their deep suffering. There were some who had made up their minds that when the *Mayflower* set sail again for England, they would be returning with her.

Although early in the morning, the village was already astir. Smoke from cooking fires rose into the softer air, women stirred porridge, men sharpened and honed their tools in readiness for the day's work. One or two of the small children came from the houses and began to play in the dusty street. A strong keen wind had sprung up over the last week, which had dried the winter mud and enabled the planting of corn kernels for a hopeful early crop. Up in the fort, the military men were about their business of cleaning the great guns brought from the ship and posted on the roof.

From the Governor's hut, Tom saw Elizabeth Tilley emerge, carrying two empty buckets, and begin to climb the hill towards him. Tom, about to pick up his own water pails, hesitated for a moment. The water was needed in the Brewster home, Mistress Brewster had urged him to make haste, and already he had dawdled and wasted some time. Well, he thought he'd wait another moment or two. He rather liked Elizabeth; she was pretty, merry and liked a joke and a bit of gossip, now that she was getting used to the loss of her parents. Two small cousins of hers, Henry Samson and Humility Cooper, had also lost their families to the sickness and been left alone in the world. The governor, John Carver and his wife, having no children of their own, had taken the three into their own hearts and home.

Tom thought that Elizabeth was the kind of girl he might marry when he grew up, if he had to get married at all, which he rather hoped he might avoid. Girls in general were inclined to be silly, but he supposed he would need someone to wash and clean for him when he became a man, and Elizabeth was different from most.

He watched Elizabeth start up the street and then suddenly stop. One of the wooden buckets fell from her hand with a thud. She was staring up the street, towards the pool, the fort and the forest. Then she turned and ran back towards the Carvers' house, her petticoats swinging and the bucket bumping against her legs.

Tom's mouth fell open in surprise. Elizabeth looked as though she'd seen something that frightened her almost speechless. He felt his own skin prickle with alarm. Had she seen a bear coming out of the woods? Bears came out of their winter sleep in the spring, he'd been told, and when they did they were very hungry and very bad-tempered. Should he run for it, or were you not supposed to run from bears? Slowly, he turned his head.

There, standing at the edge of the trees under the hemlocks and spruces, not more than a stone's throw away from him, was a tall Indian man with long black hair. He wore only a leather skin on a thong about his waist and was armed with a bow and a full quiver of arrows. This was no small brown-skinned boy, but a hard-muscled, stony-faced warrior. For a moment the small boy and tall man stared into each other's eyes. The Indian's eyes were dark and mysterious as deep pools. Then, without a word, the brown-skinned man moved out from under the cover of the trees and walked in long loping strides to the common-house.

Tom's heart was thumping hard. He grabbed his water buckets and ran down the hill, water sloshing out at every step. In the village, people were coming out of their huts and staring. The men grabbed muskets and set off towards the common-house. "Indians!" was the word on every lip.

Mistress Brewster tried to calm the children and bring back normality to the day. She took the buckets from Tom, tut-tutting at the amount he had spilled, and told the boys to collect an armful of wood and chips for the fires.

"All this fuss! It's not a war party, just one Indian! Let the men deal with him, and let us tend to our own business."

The other boys were clustering round Tom, buzzing with questions.

"Did he speak to you?"

"Were you scared?"

"Did he have warpaint on?"

"Is he going to kill us, do you think?"

"Let's go up and see what's happening!"

This last suggestion was too tempting to resist. The whole gang of boys hastily dumped on the pile the wood they'd gathered and headed up the hill to the common-house. There they soon discovered a gap in the chinking through which they could peer into the dim interior.

The men had met the tall Indian, who now stood inside, arms folded, face expressionless. A group of the leaders stood facing him, some looking a great deal more flustered than the Indian, who looked calmly into their faces. Then he said, in English, "Welcome, strangers. I come in peace. My name is Samoset."

***

They learned that Samoset was from the tribe of Massasoit, several days' walk to the north. He had picked up the English language from the traders and fishermen who landed near his tribal grounds in the summer months. He had been sent to enquire of the Pilgrims what their intentions were, as it had become apparent that they meant to stay and settle here.

Fear and distrust eased as the men talked together, although Miles Standish still frowned a little and fingered his musket. He had a deep distrust of Indians, even one who came alone, in peace, and speaking his own language.

Samoset said that the tribe who had lived here had been the Patuxet, who had been completely wiped out by a strange disease some years ago. So that explained the mysterious village of the dead. He told them that his tribe would help the settlers and would live at peace with them. The faces of Governor Carver and William Bradford lit up, and William Brewster muttered, "Praise be to God!" Captain Standish tugged at his beard and his frown deepened. He would not be so easily convinced.

At noon, the women prepared food and the Indian ate with the rest of them. A couple of wild ducks had been shot the day before and were roasted over the fire, and they made fresh biscuits and brought out some of the last remaining precious cheese and butter. Samoset ate heartily, sitting cross-legged on the ground, quite unperturbed by the curious stares of the children and the shy glances of the women. His hair was long and coarse, black as night, hanging down his back under a leather band about his brow. Moccasins were on his feet, but he was quite naked apart from the leather cloth about his waist. He had laid his bow and quiver down beside him, and Francis Billington fingered the flight of an arrow until a cuff from his father obliged him to stop.

"Isn't he cold, in this cutting wind?" whispered Mary Brewster to her husband. William agreed, or maybe he considered the Indian's clothing far too immodest to be acceptable. At any rate, he found a coat from his own chest and offered it to Samoset, who seemed delighted and put it on at once. He seemed very pleased to be in their midst, and as the afternoon wore on showed no signs of leaving the village. The Pilgrim leaders looked at one another. They were uneasy at the thought of a native

Indian among them overnight; despite their faith and the words of peace spoken by the man. Doubts hovered in their minds. What if he scalped them as they slept? Or stole their precious tools and goods? Hadn't they had thefts of tools while they worked in the woods? Or he might even make off with one of the small children – they'd heard plenty of tales of children stolen by Indians...

In the end, they lodged him in the household of Stephen Hopkins, where the Indian slept soundly curled up on a mat on the ground, but Stephen himself stayed awake and kept watch all night, just in case.

Chapter Thirteen

The pipe of peace

Next day, Samoset went on his way, looking pleased with the parting gifts he had been given from the belongings of the settlers – a knife, a bead bracelet and a ring. However, the following day he was back again, bringing with him five other Indians, all tall, dark-haired, swarthy men in leather moccasins and leggings. This time they carried no bows and arrows with them. Samoset told the Pilgrim leaders that they had left their weapons at a distance of a quarter of a mile or so. Instead, they carried over their arms the rich pelts of beavers.

"We trade," said Samoset to Governor Carver.

It was a Sunday, and the Pilgrims had been at their morning prayers and preaching when the Indians walked into the village. A flicker of alarm had gone through the company when they saw them coming, but William Brewster had calmed them with a few well-chosen words. The Indians stood and listened respectfully until the prayers were done.

But trading on the Sabbath was another matter. Governor Carver and Elder Brewster explained as best they could that this was a special day kept for worshipping God, but that they were welcome to stay or bring more furs to trade another day.

Around the cooking fires, the women exchanged glances. As a special concession to their guests, the women were to be allowed to cook on the Sabbath.

"Though how we shall manage, with six extra mouths to feed, I cannot think," muttered Mistress Hopkins, and several of the others agreed. Nevertheless, there were some fresh-caught fish and eels, and a couple of wild duck hanging from a beam that could be quickly plucked and dressed, and they were used to eking out what supplies they had with whatever was available. The Indians ate well, none could argue with that. They seemed to have the idea that the *Mayflower* was a source of unlimited stores and supplies.

After the meal, the men got down to the business of discussing future plans. Tom and the others hung around, fascinated by the tall strange men and not wanting to miss a thing. They learned that the tribe's leader was called Massasoit, and that there was another man, called Squanto, who spoke even better English than Samoset and would be willing to come and help the Pilgrims and act as interpreter.

The Indians left later that day, and the Pilgrims prepared for the evening devotions. William Brewster addressed the gathering.

"Let us offer our thanks for the happenings of this day. It has pleased God to send help to us in the form of these native men, and it is nothing short of a miracle that some can speak to us in our own tongue. Truly our God is the one who can do more than we can ask or even think."

There were some mutterings among the Strangers, the ship's crew and soldiers, who during the terrible winter had joined the Pilgrims at their prayers and worship, seeming to find comfort in their steadfast hope and trust. They had been encouraged to add their voices to the discussions that often freely accompanied the worship. Now Captain Standish spoke. "How do we know that we can trust these red men? What guarantee do we have of their goodwill?"

"None," said William Brewster quietly. "But we do have a choice. We can choose to view the words of these men with suspicion and distrust and so increase the differences between us and encourage enmity, which in our situation we can sore afford. Or, we can choose to trust, to take them at their word, to promote friendship between our people and theirs, and in doing so benefit both ourselves and them. It may even be that our godly example might awaken a desire to know for themselves the God to whom we belong."

More murmuring was heard, both of agreement and dissent.

"What about those tools they stole from us? And those arrows fired at us that first night we spent ashore?" Master Billington wanted to know.

William Brewster shrugged that off. "What are a few tools? And as for the arrows – well, that attack was likely the action of men frightened and feeling under threat from something not known. And it was not here. Those men today brought no weapons."

A woman's voice spoke up, unusually for the gatherings, but these were unusual times. "I don't like it. Heathen savages, that's what they are! I'll be glad when the ship sails and I can go home."

There were others who shared that view. Now that almost all the travellers were housed ashore and the supplies brought from the ship, the *Mayflower* would soon be sailing. Several had decided that they would return with her, and others had yet to make a final decision.

As the discussion went on, Tom thought about his own situation. He knew that for him too there was a decision to be made. William Brewster had promised him a safe home if he chose to return, maybe at the big house in Scrooby where there were kind Separatist sympathisers who would take care of him. There were cheerful people like Martha and the jolly cook, and plenty of good food and a warm fire.

But then, he'd grown to like so many of the people here too. The Brewsters had been like parents to him, the other boys were good company, even the Billington boys with their tendency to bullying and mischief. He liked Priscilla and John Alden and Elizabeth, he was getting good at fishing, and he loved the woods now that they were fresh green and teeming with life...

He was torn between the two, not knowing which to choose. The Pilgrims must choose to trust the Indians or not, and he, Tom Turner, had his own choices to make.

A few days later, the Indians were back again, the same four or five men, who said that their chief and others were waiting nearby to see if the settlers wished to parley with them. They had brought with them the stolen tools, which Samoset handed over solemnly to Governor Carver. Tom saw the face of William Brewster light up. This was the sign he had prayed for, the sign of honesty and goodwill that would maybe convince those who doubted. The meeting was arranged, and Samoset was sent back with messages of welcome and gifts of knives, beads and some of the carefully hoarded cheese and butter from the stores.

Early in the afternoon, Tom and Richard were helping with fetching and carrying for the men working on a house and, in between, learning from John Alden to carefully shape the wooden pegs for fastening wood to beams. Suddenly John paused, looked up the street and dropped his hammer with a clatter. At the top of the hill, on the banks of the Town Brook, a party of Indians had emerged from the trees and was gazing down at the village. They stood motionless, twenty or more men, and Tom could see from their heads the flutter of feathers in the breeze. Hammering and sawing had stopped, a hush fell over the community, and for a few minutes the two groups stood silent and still, neither making any move towards the other. Then one of the Indians detached himself from the group, crossed the stream and walked down into the village. This man had a large, prominent nose, a strong chin and head shaved except for a thick tuft of hair on top. Round his neck was a necklace of shells. The two men nearest, Governor Carver and Edward Winslow, stepped forward. Could this be the chief? But the Indian stopped as he reached them and said, in excellent English, "Good day. I am Squanto. I am to be your interpreter."

Greetings were exchanged. Squanto, it seemed, had belonged to the tragic Patuxet tribe and was in fact their only survivor, having been captured by slave traders and taken to Spain and England where he had remained for several years before returning. He was now prepared to act as go-between for the Massasoit and the settlers. He said that Chief Massasoit awaited beyond the stream and would speak with the leaders, would trade with them and live in peace.

This was to be no casual meeting, but one of solemn importance, or so the settlers soon realised. Governor Carver quickly instructed his wife and the other women to go to his own house, spread a rug on the floor and place some comfortable pillows on it. A welcoming party, led by Miles Standish, went to the stream bank with Squanto and then conducted Chief Massasoit to the house, where he was met by the Governor and the other leaders. The sight of the chief caused everyone to stare, and some of the smaller children hid behind the skirts of their mothers. The chief's head and face glistened with oil, his face was decorated with red paint and a long necklace of white bone beads swung around his neck. His hair was decorated with feathers and his leather leggings with coloured beads. He and some of his men disappeared into the new timber house, and a low hum of voices from within sounded all through the afternoon.

As the day wore on towards dusk, the fires were stoked and the women once again stretched their supplies to feed many mouths, thankful that there was venison and game from the woods and fish from the bay. The visitors grew relaxed and, when they had eaten, showed their thanks by performing a tribal dance for the entertainment of their hosts, shuffling their feet and twisting their hands in elaborate movements as they moved in a circle. The children lost their fear and clapped in time. One of the Indians showed an interest in the soldiers' trumpet and tried to blow it, without much success. They murmured in admiration as the trumpeter played a rousing tune.

Towards evening, Massasoit produced tobacco and a pipe and proposed that he and the white men smoke it together as a sign of peace between their peoples. The smoke curled upwards into the spring dusk, and the settlers felt a new, frail but hopeful sense of new beginnings, of fresh opportunities, of purpose and freedom.

Chapter Fourteen

The coming of spring

Once more, a funeral procession was wending its way to Burial Hill. This time it was Elizabeth, the wife of Edward Winslow, who was being laid to rest, having succumbed to the racking cough and lingering weakness brought on by the rigours of the hard voyage and harder winter. Despite the greening of the forest and the coming of spring, almost a dozen people had died that month alone. The only difference with this burial was that now, with the peace treaty and smoking of the peace pipe, the interment could take place in full daylight.

Afterwards, the young widower made his way back to the village, to be comforted as best as was possible by so many others who had lost loved ones in that harsh and terrible time. And then the work of building and planting must go on.

The sailors had rowed the last of the supplies over from the ship that very morning, and in just a few days' time the *Mayflower* would be homeward bound. Those who wished to return would say their farewells and board the ship for the journey home.

Tom's mind was still in turmoil. On hard days, with his skin chapped and red raw, his muscles aching from digging and raking soil, his stomach crying out for the fresh milk, cream, butter, eggs, fresh bread and fruit of England, his whole body shivering from the cutting winds that blew through every crack in the rough houses, he longed for the old country. At other times, even a glimpse of a violet or a buttercup pushing up from the detritus of winter, or the sound of small children laughing as they ran on the beach, or one of the men giving him a 'Well done!' after some piece of finished work, could set him thinking that life could be good and maybe he could belong here in this new world.

He wished there was someone to tell him how to decide, to make the way clear and plain for him. He knew that the Pilgrims prayed to God for help and guidance in their decisions. But something seemed to hold him back from asking them to pray for him too. Sometimes, in spite of the kindness shown to him, he felt alone, belonging nowhere.

The men had gone back to their planting and their building. The other big boys were off into the forest, catapults in hand, hoping for a rabbit or a squirrel. They were more confident now, learning how to tread silently along the winding paths, knowing how to approach downwind from their prey, becoming wise in the ways of the wilderness. Squanto was teaching them tracking skills, among other things, and the boys hung on his every word. There were still some among the settlers who were uneasy at the thought of an Indian moving freely among them, some who hurried into their houses when he was near. But most could see the value of his help and advice and thanked God for it.

For some reason, Tom had felt reluctant to go with the other boys that afternoon. Instead, he took a bucket and headed for the beach. There, at certain times, the sand was littered with tiny dead fish, washed up and often stinking when they began to rot. They had been surprised when one day Squanto brought a bucketful of these tiny, stinking fish into the village.

"He can't mean we're to eat them, can he?" asked Mistress Hopkins, aghast.

"Nothing would surprise me about those heathens," said Mistress Billington with a sniff.

But the small fish were not for food. Instead, Squanto showed them how they could be used as fertiliser. When the next corn crop was planted, he demonstrated the way the Indians did it. Deftly, he formed a small hillock of soil from the cleared and cultivated ground, pushed four kernels of corn into the middle of it, added several small fish and covered it all with more soil. He moved swiftly along the rows, repeating this action time and again – hillock, seed, fish, soil.

"Well I'm blessed!" said Governor Carver admiringly. "That is something we'd never have thought of for ourselves. Maybe our spring crops will do better than the winter ones."

The winter crops, barley and rye, were coming up sparse and not as healthy-looking as they would have wished. Everyone worked with a will on the spring crops: the governor, the elders and leaders, the girls and women too whenever they could be spared from their household tasks. Corn, peas and beans were planted in long rows. And the children did their part by collecting the smelly fish-fertiliser from the beach.

Today, though, there seemed to be few fish washed up and stranded on the beach. The sea was calm, and out in the bay the *Mayflower* rocked gently at anchor, riding high in the water now that she was lightened of her passengers and cargo. In another few days she would be gone, heading back for the old world, and with her would go the last link with that world for the settlers.

Tom walked slowly along the deserted beach, head down, heart heavy with the weight of the decision that had to be made. The tide was coming in, lapping gently nearer and nearer to his feet. Suddenly, he caught a glimpse of white among the rocks at the highest point of the beach, where the lush vegetation reached down to the shore. It moved slightly, and he saw that it was the white cap of one of the women. Someone was sitting there alone among the rocks, and as he approached he heard another sound mingling with the gentle hiss and ripple of the waves – the sound of soft weeping.

Tom stopped in his tracks. The death of Dorothy Bradford was still clear in his mind. In general, the Pilgrim women seldom wept. They scolded, admonished, encouraged, and sometimes, it had to be said, gossiped and speculated. The girls shrieked and giggled and were sometimes reprimanded for it. He had seen tears pour silently down the faces of men, women and children as they stood at the gravesides of loved ones. But, apart from tragic Dorothy Bradford, he had never before seen one of them sitting weeping alone.

He turned to retrace his steps. He had not been able to help Dorothy, but maybe he could fetch someone who would help this woman. But just then the white bonnet turned, and he saw beneath it the tear-streaked face of Priscilla Mullins. He stopped again, not knowing whether to go or stay. But Priscilla called out to him, "Tom! Is that you? Don't run away."

Tom awkwardly came forward, setting down his pail. Priscilla wrinkled her nose. "You're collecting fish. Ugh!"

Tom pulled a face too. Even with the few fish he'd found, the smell was strong and had a way of sticking to hands and clothes and hair.

Priscilla said, "Never mind. I can bear it. Come and sit down."

Tom perched on a rock. Tendrils of dark hair were escaping from her cap and her face was flushed and tear-stained. She sighed and said, "Oh, Tom. Life is hard sometimes, is it not? Hard to know the way forward..."

Tom nodded. This was exactly how he felt himself. He remembered that Priscilla had lost her whole family, her mother and father and her brother Joseph, who had been his own good friend and playmate. She was quite alone in the world.

Priscilla sighed again, clasping her arms round her knees beneath the long grey skirts of her woollen dress and staring out to sea. She said, "I have been asking God to show me the way forward, whether I should stay here or return with the ship. I have relatives in England who I know would take me in. But – as yet there is no clear answer. I'm still not sure..."

Tom was startled. "Asking God?"

She turned to look at him. "Yes. That is the only sure way of finding guidance for my life."

"But – can you ask him yourself then? I thought – I thought – it was only Elder Brewster and the other leaders who could pray to God..."

Priscilla smiled gently and tucked a stray wisp of hair under her cap. Her tears had dried and she seemed more like her usual cheerful self now. She said, "No, no. Any one of us, man, woman or child, can come to God and ask him freely whatever we will. That is why his Son Jesus died, so that our sins could be washed clean and every one of us have a way into his holy presence. That is why we came here to this place, to be able to come freely before God and worship without ritual devised by man."

"And – does he answer?"

"Oh, yes! Not always in words, but always at the right time, in the right way, when he wills. He knows far better than we know and answers accordingly."

Tom was silent, digesting this information. If anyone could ask God for help, then – did that mean he could too? Even though he was not really one of the Pilgrims? Did God's love reach to him too?

Priscilla looked at him, seemingly able to read his thoughts. She said, "Yes, you too, Tom. You can ask God anything you desire. He loves you and will answer you."

Tom felt a heaviness lift from his heart. God would help him and guide him! He only had to ask. Because God loved him – *him*, Tom Turner, who belonged to no one. Maybe he could belong after all, to the settlers and to God. And if he belonged, the hard work, the harsh weather, the disappointments and discouragements could be borne, because he would be sharing them with people who loved and cared.

Priscilla reached out and squeezed his hand, then got to her feet, smoothing down her grey skirts and white apron. "I must get back to my work. Thank you, Tom Turner."

"For what?"

"For happening by. Speaking to you has eased my heart and restored my faith. Now, I think I see what God is saying to me. I think I understand at last what he has been speaking to my heart these past few weeks—"

"And you'll be staying?"

She nodded, her eyes bright again. "I think I will be staying. One or two things need to be settled." She smiled, and her cheeks were suddenly as pink as a wild rose. She said, "And may God guide you too, Tom Turner." And then she was gone, tripping lightly across the sand as though she had not a care in the world.

Tom watched her go, and then turned again to look at the ship, rocking lightly at anchor. He thought he now knew what his own decision would be.

But maybe not his decision alone. He turned his face up to the evening sky and said aloud, "God, I never knew I could ask you to help me. But I'm asking you now, so please let me do what is right. And help me to know you better."

Chapter Fifteen

Farewell to the Mayflower

Two days later, in the first week of April, the *Mayflower* sailed on the morning tide.

For several days there had been great activity in the Pilgrim village, as messages were composed and letters written to be carried back over the sea and delivered to families in the old world. Those who could write were in great demand by those who could not, and William Brewster in particular spent many hours with quill in hand faithfully setting down the messages he had been asked to record. Many lists were made, of goods to be sent to the New World when a ship visited its shores again. More tools were needed, seed, livestock, in particular a cow or two would be of enormous benefit to the community, warm clothing, bedding, sewing materials, shoes. Every day more items were added to the list. Then there were reports of the voyage to be written for the shipping masters, and trading options must be presented for discussion and decision. After a day's work in the fields, William Brewster and a few others often sat far into the night, writing by candlelight.

The leaders had reckoned that in time, good supplies of furs and pelts could be purchased from the Indians, therefore goods for bartering must be added to the lists too – beads, knives, trinkets, clothing and certain foodstuffs and medicines were what Massasoit and his people had asked for. The lists seemed endless.

The morning of departure dawned clear and bright, blue smoke rising into the air from among the thatched roofs of the village. Inside, all was hustle and bustle with last preparations. The ship's captain, Christopher Jones, was impatient to be gone before the tide turned or the fair wind shifted back to the east, but he had come ashore to collect the last of the letters and messages and to share in the farewell prayers and blessings of the Pilgrims.

The whole population of the village and the ship – Separatists, Strangers, soldiers and seamen – stood together one last time on the beach near the bay. A stiff breeze flapped the torn and patched sails of the *Mayflower*, waiting across the water, and ruffled the hair of the children and the skirts of the women. Tom stood with the Brewster family and felt the hand of little Wrestling creep into his own. Even the smallest children felt the solemnity of the occasion.

That morning, Elder Brewster had taken Tom aside for a moment and looked at him keenly from his clear grey eyes. "Are you quite sure now, Tom?"

Tom had nodded and said, "Yes, sir. Quite sure."

And the doubts had gone, disappearing like morning mist in the early sunshine. God had answered his prayers, and he knew without further doubt where his future would be. And when the prayers had been offered, with Godspeed for the return voyage, he added his own 'Amen' to the chorus that went up from the assembled group.

The captain jumped into the waiting boat and the creaking of oars mingled with the splash of waves as he was rowed to his waiting vessel. Those on shore stood in silence and watched the tiny figures of sailors heaving on the windlass to raise the anchor. The yardarm was braced, sails set to the west and soon the *Mayflower* was moving away, out of the shelter of the bay. The watchers on shore saw her round the point and watched the wind fill her sails as she stood for the open Atlantic Ocean. Then the sails were growing smaller, a white dot in a vast sea of blue.

A chorus of sighs went up from the people on the beach. For good or ill, their last link with the old world had disappeared over the horizon. In ones and twos they began to make their way back up to the village, to their digging and hoeing, their carpentry, cooking and care of the babies, the myriad of other tasks to be done. Tom noticed that Priscilla Mullins walked with John Alden, his fair head bent low to her white-capped one as they talked together in low tones. The day before, they had announced their intention of being joined in marriage as soon as it could be arranged.

That morning, Priscilla had beckoned Tom aside as he passed with wood for the fire. "Tom! I wish you to be the first to hear my good tidings! The dear Lord has answered my prayers in such a way that cannot be mistaken!"

Her cheeks had grown as pink as the crab apple blossom just bursting its buds in the thicket beyond the village. "John – that is, John Alden, has asked me to be his wife! And I have accepted! The elders have given us their blessing."

Tom had felt his heart give a joyful leap. This pair were two of his favourite people. But he was a little puzzled too. "But – John is a crewman, is he not? He is not one of the Pilgrims. Will he not be returning with the ship when she sails?"

She shook her head, eyes dancing like sunbeams. "No. That is the best of all! John has decided that he will throw in his lot with us here at Plymouth! He will be of great help in the work here. He has himself come to faith in God, and in his son Jesus! Oh, I am so happy!"

She almost danced away back to her household tasks.

Tom could not help but be happy too. Since he had made his own decision to stay, a quiet peace and confidence had filled his heart. He now felt he truly belonged.

In the end, the challenge and promise of the New World had proved stronger than the pull of the old. Not one of the settlers, Stranger or Pilgrim, had chosen to return on the *Mayflower*.

***

*E*ven now, with spring here and romance in the air, the Plymouth village was not finished with tragedy. Just a few days after the sailing of the *Mayflower*, something happened that once again shook them to the core. There had come a warm, sunny spell, bees buzzed in the wild cherry and crab apple blossom and everyone worked with a will in the corn patch and vegetable garden. Governor Carver did his full share, digging, planting and hoeing with the rest. But at noon one day, with the sun hot overhead, he slumped to the ground where he had been plying his hoe between the hopeful rows of peas and beans, and lay still. Others rushed to help him rise, but he had been so badly stricken that he could barely move. Four men carried him to his house, but he never spoke or rose from his bed again, and in a few days was dead.

The company was shocked and saddened. And the shock doubled when, in just a few more days, the Governor's wife Mary, never strong since the winter sickness, became sick and died also. Some said that her heart was broken, her will to live gone. The villagers felt a double sense of bereavement as they laid Mary to rest beside her husband at the edge of the field of sprouting green corn.

Now the Pilgrims had no governor. And looking at the saddened faces around the graveside, trying to take hope from Elder Brewster's words from the Scriptures, Tom suddenly realised something else. Opposite him stood Elizabeth Tilley, with her small cousins Henry and Humility clutching tight to her skirts. The tears were pouring down Elizabeth's face. Two months before, when her mother died, John and Mary Carver had taken in the three children and given them a home. Now, once again, they were without home or family.

There was some discussion as to the future of the three children. It was suggested that they be divided up among the families, as Elizabeth was far too young to be solely responsible for the two little ones. But Henry and Humility, bewildered and frightened by this fresh loss, clung tightly to their cousin and cried bitterly at the thought of being separated.

In the end, it was the big-hearted William Brewster who once more came to the rescue. "Mary, can we not make a little more space to accommodate these three?"

Mary, with her usual motherly warmth, assured him that they could.

But when the children had collected their few belongings and brought them to the Brewster house, it seemed crowded indeed. The house was one of the biggest in the village but now would be crammed full to overflowing with no less than seven children. Where they would all sleep was something of a puzzle. Wrestling had his little trundle bed tucked away under the big bed of his parents, and the other three boys slept on pallets on the floor. More beds would be made at some stage, but were not considered a priority in these busy days of spring. The rest of the space seemed already full, with a table, a big chair for the master of the house, a stool for Mary and the various boxes, chests and trunks containing their possessions from the old world. Tom knew that one of the chests was filled completely with books, for Elder Brewster was a great scholar.

William Brewster stroked his whiskers and considered the situation. He said, "I think a sleeping loft may provide a solution. I shall consult John Alden, who is handy with the carpentry, and thank God we have no shortage of wood with the forest on our very doorstep.

It would take but a day or two to construct, with a ladder to reach it. Then these rascally boys can sleep above, and Elizabeth and the little ones stay below."

Everyone approved of this idea, the boys most of all. It would be fun to have their own sleeping space high up among the roof beams under the thatch. All kinds of possibilities for entertainment flitted through their minds – objects could be dropped on unsuspecting people below, forbidden catapults and blowpipes hidden up above and aimed wherever they chose, if they were careful. And Tom was glad that pretty Elizabeth and her little cousins were going to share his home.

The next pressing need was the appointing of a new governor. Several meetings were held in the big meeting-room at the top of the hill, under the look-out point where Miles Standish and his men had their big guns. Very soon, a unanimous decision had been reached and was announced to the rest of the settlers. William Bradford would now be Governor of Plymouth Village.

Chapter Sixteen

A celebration

A beautiful morning in early summer dawned over Plymouth village, where a great bustle of preparation had begun almost before the first rays of sun had slanted down through the forest. Today there would be a wedding, the first in the new colony. Edward Winslow and Susanna White were to be joined in marriage, and everyone rejoiced. Two grief-stricken people would find comfort and companionship, and two small boys would not grow up fatherless. After all the hardships, the loss and bitter disappointments of the past months, planning a joyful occasion such as this put new hope in the hearts and a new spring in the step of everyone in the village.

Since early morning the children had been busy, gathering fragrant pine boughs, flowering May blossom thick with creamy-white flowers and twining strands of honeysuckle to make a sweet-smelling bower under which the bride and groom would stand to make their vows. In the homes, a feast was being prepared: duck and venison, hare and fish, with pastries and sweetmeats made from the carefully hoarded supplies and the first tender young vegetables of the season.

The ceremony was a short and simple one. The couple made their vows before the Governor and Elder Brewster offered thanks and gave a short homily on the blessing and sanctity of marriage. Among the gathered people, John Alden and Priscilla Mullins had eyes only for one another and dreamed of their own wedding day. The newly married pair accepted the well-wishes of the people with thankful hearts, their recent sharp grief and loss turned into renewed hope for the future.

After the ceremony, the feast was to be served out of doors, and all the tables in the village had been brought out and placed together along the village street. There had been one or two who questioned such a lavish celebration, considering how recently the new bride and groom had been widow and widower. But the leaders wisely saw the need for a time of rejoicing; an interlude from unceasing toil in which to laugh and dance, eat and drink and look to the future. The whole village had looked forward to this day.

Already the tables groaned with good things, and more dishes were being brought out of the houses. The boys stood staring with undisguised greed. It was many months since such a plentiful sight had met their eyes.

"Do not touch a thing until thanks have been offered!" warned Mistress Hopkins, brandishing a wooden spoon in their direction. She would use it, too, as several of them knew to their discomfort, having had their knuckles skinned by that very same spoon.

"Goose *and* duck *and* jugged hare," said Love Brewster in a gloating whisper.

"And sweetmeats!" added Richard. "Real raisin pastries! I never knew we had raisins!"

There were even little, ripe, wild strawberries set along the tables in temptingly piled dishes. They grew in profusion along the banks of the Town Brook, and the girls had spent hours the day before picking the tiny jewel-like fruit. Tom felt his mouth water. But they all had to wait as the new husband and wife and then the heads of the households were seated in the wooden chairs. Until there was time to make more, one chair per household was the rule, and it was the man who sat in it. Some of the women had stools, and there were long forms for the children in some of the houses. But mostly the children stood to eat, using fingers as often as spoons to feed themselves.

The grace was said and food passed around. The food began to vanish like fat on a hot skillet, as Mistress Brewster remarked. Laughter pealed along the village street and later there would be music and dancing, with the trumpets and horns of the military men pressed into service. Below them, the white-capped waves danced on a blue sea; above, the pines and hemlocks whispered gently in a soft breeze.

Elizabeth Tilley had a slightly wistful look on her face. "Do you think heaven will be like this?" she asked, as Tom passed with yet another pastry in his hand.

He stopped with the pastry halfway to his lips. He'd never really thought much about heaven, though he supposed that so many of the Pilgrims and his own mother must be there. He had been told heaven was a wonderful place, and looking at the sparkling water, the swaying branches and feeling the sun warm on his face, he couldn't imagine anything more wonderful than this.

"I think it may be," he said, and thought for a moment of his mother, and Elizabeth's, and all the people who had sailed on the *Mayflower* and never lived to see this day.

There was a sudden shout from Samuel Fuller, at the top of the path leading down to the shore. "A boat! There's a boat coming!"

A ripple of excitement ran up and down the village street. No boats had come near over the whole of the long winter. The tables were nearly abandoned and there was a rush of feet to the path, and people shaded their eyes against the sun to see for themselves. Sure enough, a shallop with several men was heading into the bay, and beyond, a larger ship stood at anchor.

Several of the men went down to the shore to greet the newcomers. The boys felt themselves torn, not wanting to miss any excitement, but on the other hand, if they left the feast, the good things might have disappeared by the time they returned. They decided to stay near the provisions, just in case. And maybe they could help themselves to a little extra while attention was elsewhere.

Soon the men returned, with three or four sailors carrying casks, which some of them carried up to the pool in the Town Brook. They had put in to replenish their fresh water supplies, they said. Their vessel was called the *White Gull*, a trading ship. They had heard of this colony and were curious to know how it was faring, and were rather surprised to find a marriage feast in progress. And there was something else...

Tom suddenly felt a strange prickling sensation in his scalp, as if insects crawled in his hair. One of the sailors was deep in conversation with Elder Brewster and Governor Bradford, and then all three turned towards Tom and looked at him strangely. The sailor turned away down the path towards the shore, and the two leaders came across to where Tom stood. He looked from one face to another, wondering at their expressions, both serious and surprised.

William Brewster cleared his throat. "Tom, that fellow had news concerning you. He said that there is a crewman aboard the *White Gull*, a cooper by the name of Thomas Turner. This man has been enquiring whether there is here with us a boy of the same name."

Tom felt the blood drain from his face and a dizziness come over him. His thoughts whirled. It could not be! And yet – and yet – it must be, the name, the trade, the searching for a boy – it was all too much to be coincidence. His father was alive, had traced him to this place, was here, and was asking for him.

A confusion of thoughts filled his mind, one question coming so hard upon the heels of another that they tumbled over themselves. Why had his father come searching now, when his mother was dead and beyond help? If it had been sooner he might perhaps have saved her, or at least eased her heart. Why had he come here?

He swayed a little on his feet and William Brewster put out a hand to steady him.

"Tom? Are you faint? This has been a shock to you, I fear. This man would appear to be your long-lost father. Do you wish to meet with him?"

"Is – is he on the ship?"

"He's here, down on the beach, waiting. You need not see him if that is not your wish, Tom. Or, I will gladly go with you and see what he has to say."

Tom felt the tears spring to his eyes at the kindly words and the concern in the eyes of this man who, despite his own family and heavy responsibilities, had always made Tom feel that he was of great value and mattered much. He had been the best of fathers himself to Tom, ever since the day they had ridden together into

Scrooby on the back of the post horse. Tom knew that, if he wished, Elder Brewster would turn Thomas Turner away and keep him, Tom, in his own family.

For a moment he was tempted. Then he said, "I will see him. And I'll go alone."

He straightened his shoulders and left the two leaders, walking determinedly down to the beach, though under him his legs were shaking. Behind, in the village, the musicians among the settlers were assembling for the music and dancing to come. On the beach, the sailors were loading their casks into the shallop and pausing to smoke their pipes before pushing off. In the shade of the trees overhanging the rocks where the forest met the shore, another man was standing alone.

Chapter Seventeen

New beginnings

For a moment, the shape of the man, dark against the dazzle of bright sunshine on water, seemed familiar to Tom. Then he thought he must be mistaken. This man was much older than he remembered, with grey streaks in his beard and in the hair showing under the stocking cap he wore. The face was tanned and deeply lined, the mouth unsmiling and set. But then Tom saw the eyes, deep-set and hazel, his own eyes, and he knew that this was indeed the father he had not seen for more than three years.

He stopped. The man looked keenly at him and held out his hand.

"Tom? Can this be you? You are so much altered, taller, thinner too—"

Tom swallowed a gulp and said, "We are all thin here." Even as he spoke, he realised what a foolish kind of greeting this sounded. But the man nodded.

"Yes. I understand you have all suffered much."

Sudden anger rose and filled Tom's heart. He thought - you understand nothing! You left us to fend for ourselves and broke my mother's heart... He said aloud,

150

the anger bursting forth into words, "Why did you leave us? My mother is dead! She was sick for a long time and you cared nothing!"

The man made a step towards him, holding out his hand as though to ward off a blow. Tom backed a few steps away. His father said, "Tom, I have come to ask your forgiveness. I have no excuse for my action, save that I could not bear the pain in your mother's face, the sadness and grief, the knowing that nothing I could do would ease it. I took the coward's way. Yet I always intended to return, to make things right for her again, to start afresh." A pleading, desperate note had come into his voice.

Tom hardened his heart. "It's too late now. She's dead, and I live here, with my friends."

The man sighed. He looked out to sea, where the *White Gull* rocked gently on the waves. "I am so sorry, Tom. For a while I sought to put my family far from my mind, drowning my memories with strong drink. Then I met a man, a man very much like your Separatist friends, who led me by his example to see how wrong I had been, and also that there was forgiveness for me in Christ. I have found that forgiveness. I sought at once to make amends, only to find your mother in her grave and you gone.

I remembered her childhood home at Scrooby, went to enquire there and they told me at the old Post House where you had gone. I took passage on the first ship I could find which might land me on these shores. I had to find you, Tom."

Tom was silent, his mind a turmoil of confused thoughts. His father had sought him to ask his forgiveness. Well, he wasn't sure that he was able to forgive him, or that he deserved forgiveness. Why should he not suffer as he and his mother had suffered?

Up in the village, the music had begun and sounds of laughter and merrymaking floated down. Tom said, "I have to go. It is a wedding feast. There are those who will wonder where I am."

He half-turned to go. His father moved as though to stop him but then stepped back, a sadness deepening the lines of his face. "I have no right to try to detain you, Tom. He paused and said, "The ship will sail tomorrow. I will come again in the boat early in the morning and hope to speak with you again. I pray you may find it in your heart to forgive me and allow me to make amends for the past."

Tom did not stop to see him go to the boat. He fled up the path but, instead of turning into the village, plunged aside into the leafy depths of the forest, where he ran until he was exhausted and then sank onto the soft leaf-mould and sobbed and sobbed.

He must have slept, for dusk was beginning to fall when he awoke, stiff and cramped. He looked up into the dim greenness where vines twined among the new green buds of early summer and the air was sweet with the scents of honeysuckle and wild roses. In the fall, Squanto had told them, there would be grapes on the vines and that the red hips that came after the roses made a cordial, excellent for keeping away the scurvy, the disease which had hastened the deaths of so many of the settlers. Tom had looked forward to gathering these and all the other fruits that could be found in the forest. Maybe he would meet again the boy who had helped with his last berry-picking.

And now...

With a sick, empty feeling inside him he got up and made his way back to the village. The street was quiet now, the merrymaking done, tables cleared and each family gone to their own home. Tom went to the Brewster cabin and let himself in. Mary Brewster was lighting the lamp, while Elizabeth sat on the stool with a great pile of mending beside her. The little ones were already growing drowsy and Love was watching Richard whittle at a piece of wood. Love was loudly complaining of a bellyache, and his mother was telling him it was no wonder, the amount of food he had stuffed himself with, and that she had a mind to dose them all with a good spoonful of physick... William Brewster sat at the table, his Bible open before him. It all seemed homely and familiar, the grown-ups greeted him kindly and Mary

Brewster asked if he would like something to eat. He shook his head and headed straight up the ladder to the sleeping loft, where he dropped into his usual place under the eaves and pulled up the blanket.

After a while, the creaking of the ladder told that someone else was joining him in the loft. He was surprised to see the bulk of William Brewster. The Elder hardly ever came up here, but now he came over to Tom, stooping low to avoid the roof beams, and sat down stiffly beside him on Richard's sleeping pallet. Tom pretended to be asleep, keeping his eyes tightly closed, and didn't answer even when the Elder spoke his name. But he had the distinct feeling that those keen grey eyes could see, even in the darkness of the loft space; see not only his humped body but also into the very depths of his soul.

William Brewster didn't speak again, but sat quietly by Tom, resting his hand lightly on the boy's shoulder. Tom knew that he was praying. And suddenly something seemed to melt inside him, the hard knot of bitterness unravelling. In its place came the sweet sense that God knew the very worst about him and yet still loved him, that this forgiveness came because of the blood of Jesus, and that because of it he could freely forgive his own father. He sobbed quietly for a few minutes, while Elder Brewster sat quietly by and the soothing hum of everyday life sounded from the room below. Then, still without a word, William Brewster got stiffly to his feet and climbed down the ladder. Tom rubbed his tear-stained face on the blanket and then fell into a deep sleep.

***

*H*e woke as the first light filtered into the dimness of the sleeping loft. Beside him slept the humped figures of Love and Richard. Below, the rest of the large family slumbered too. Tom crept down the ladder and let himself out into the freshness of the dawn. In the bay the ship stood, ready to sail on the morning tide. It was going to be another beautiful day.

His father sat on a large rock, staring out across the bay. For a moment Tom watched in silence from the shelter of the trees, seeing the slumped shoulders, the sadness and weariness and disappointment that showed in every gesture. He came from the trees and stood beside the weary man.

"Father."

"Tom!" The man's face lit up and he jumped to his feet. They looked at each other for a moment, suddenly awkward. Then Tom said, "I'm sorry, Father, for the hard things I said. I - I will go with you, if that is what you wish."

His father seemed taken aback. "Tom, no, that is not what I came here for, to take you away. Last evening I

155

spoke with your leaders, who have cared for you so well, and they agreed that if we both wish, I can stay and work and worship here, and we can have a home together."

Tom felt his legs grow suddenly unsteady under him. He sat down on the rock where his father had been sitting. This morning, he had resolved that he would be willing to leave and go back to the old country, if his father so wished. The thought broke his heart; he realised now that he loved this place and the people here, but there had been a strange peace about the decision too.

And now there need be no sad farewells! He had made up his mind to obey God's commands, to forgive and to submit. And God had wonderfully rewarded him.

A plume of blue cooking-smoke rose above the trees, and the sounds of a child squealing with laughter and a hen cackling floated down to the shore.

Tom got up. He had missed supper and his stomach was rumbling with hunger again. "It's almost breakfast time," he said. "The hens are laying well now, and Mistress Brewster boils the eggs hard and mixes them with cooked fish. It's good! And there may be some strawberries left to go on the porridge."

He smiled at his father. His father's face broke into an answering smile, and suddenly Tom saw again a glimpse of the young man who had laughed and romped with him, who had dandled his babies upon his knees and carried his little girls upon his shoulders.

His father held out his hard, work-worn hand. Tom took it in his smaller chapped one, and together they walked up the winding path to the village, to face a new day and the beginning of the rest of their lives together in the New World.

Author's note

Tom Turner, his family and his part in the story are all imaginary. But the rest of the people in the story really lived, they sailed on the *Mayflower*, went through all the experiences in the story and settled in the new Plymouth Village in Massachusetts, USA. All the details in the story are as near as I could make them to the recorded documents.

An exact replica of the *Mayflower* was built in the twentieth century and now is anchored off Plymouth, MA. There is also a reconstruction of the Plimoth Village, sloping down to the bay where the Mayflower anchored, where actors take on the roles of the Pilgrims and dress, work, live, cook and speak in the way that the Pilgrims would have. Both the ship and the village are open to visitors and give a fascinating glimpse of the life and times of the Pilgrims.

www. plimoth.org

Bibliography

Of Plymouth Plantation, by William Bradford, Random House

Mayflower Remembered: a History of the Plymouth Pilgrims, Crispin Gill, David & Charles

New World, Judith Gunn, William Collins

The Mayflower Secret, Dave & Neta Jackson, Bethany House Publishers

Sarah Morton's Day; a Day in the Life of a Pilgrim Girl, Kate Waters, Scholastic

Samuel Eaton's Day; a Day in the Life of a Pilgrim Boy, Kate Waters, Scholastic

Tapenum's Day; a Wampanoag Indian Boy in Pilgrim Times, Kate Waters, Scholastic

If You Sailed on the Mayflower in 1620, Ann McGovern, Scholastic

Avoid Sailing on the Mayflower, Peter Cook, Book House

In the Shadow of Idris

Want a sneak preview of another *Lifepath Adventure?*
Read on for the first chapter of *In the Shadow of Idris...*

Chapter One

*H*ere comes the sun! It's floating out of the mist and warming me, up here on the Mountain. The night is over at last and I'm still alive! I'm wet and cold and I ache from lying on my bed of rock, but nothing happened. The mist is rolling away like smoke from a fire and I can see the track down to the valley below. Before I go, I want to look all ways and remember everything that I see. If I look carefully over the edge of this crag I can see, far below, the little lake that people say is bottomless. If I turn the other way I can see the great river, growing wider as it reaches the sea. I am so high! Up here I can see what the kites and buzzards see as they soar across the sky... and I'm so hungry I could eat Giant Idris for my breakfast!

She was right, of course, though there were times when I wasn't sure she would be. This was to be the big test, but she didn't make me do it. She'll most likely give me a proper telling off when she hears what I've done. But I wanted to do it. Wanted to prove to myself and all the others that what she says is true.

She's been so sure, all along the way. If she believes something she doesn't give up. Once she gets an idea in her head nothing stops her, and I should know! I can

hardly believe the things I've done because of her...
being up here, for example! I, Bryn, son of Madoc Parry
the shepherd, have spent the night alone on the seat of
Idris the Giant, in the territory of Gwyn the Hunter, and
I've come to no harm.

All my life I've lived in the shadow of the Mountain. It
looms above all the other mountains nearby and, believe
me, we have many mountains here in Wales! I grew up
knowing that it was a special mountain; a magical place
with great power. It's a place to respect and also fear. In
all weather and at all times of the year eyes are drawn to
its steep slopes and rocky crags. On the days when the
mist comes down and covers the top it's easy to believe
that something secret is going on up here. For instance,
maybe Giant Idris is tormenting some fool who has
dared to climb up and sit between the three peaks that
make his great chair. Or, on stormy nights when the
wind howls, it can sound like Gwyn the Hunter is out
rampaging with his great hounds, searching for some
unfortunate soul to drag down to the Dark Place. Oh,
there are lots of stories and many people believe them.
And, even if they don't really believe them, those stories
are useful. "Behave yourself, or the Giant will come
down the Mountain for you!"

I was fearful like all the other children but, as well as
fear, I could feel something pulling me up here. I would
look up and think. What would it be like to climb, way up

there? What would I be able to see from the top? What would happen to me? Well, now I know.

I must hurry down now, before the others start to wonder where I've gone. I must go carefully on the steep track. Mam says I'm more nimble than a mountain goat but the rocks are wet and it's easy to slip. I don't want to break my neck and be breakfast for the ravens!

1800 – a new century and a new adventure! I can't believe all that has happened to me in the past few years.

* * *

*W*e were both born here in the village, in the little valley in the mountains. Go down the wide valley with the long lake, through the big village and take the narrow track. This winds up and around the side of the hill. Keep the river beside you and you can't get lost. The hills close in and trees surround you for a while but, just around the corner, another valley opens out below. Go down, past the ruined castle on its high mound, and you're in our valley. Our village is small, with only a few families; grown-ups, children and some old people. We are all kinds; gentle and rough, clever and slow, some very strange, like Mad Bethan. We live in scattered cottages and farms. Everyone knows everyone, which can sometimes be a bit of a problem. There are more sheep than people here, that's for sure. They graze on the sides of the mountains and on the valley floor. They're everywhere!

Sometimes I think sheep are boring, stupid animals; not like Tegwyn and Bran, my Tada's dogs. But sheep are important to our village.

"Mr Rhys and his sheep keep our village alive," says my Tada. I think my father must be right because, without the sheep, Tada and the other shepherds would have no work. Without sheep there would be no wool for the women to spin into yarn, and without yarn there would be no work for the weavers. So those sheep keep most of us from going hungry.

I don't really remember noticing her until I was old enough to play with the other children, away from my own doorstep. Then I might see her in her garden or walking past our cottage with her mam. It wasn't long before I noticed that Mary, the daughter of Jacob Jones, was different. For one thing, she was cleaner than most of us. Even in winter when it's too cold to swim in the river and wash off the dust and the sheep muck that seems to stick to everything, Mary looked clean. Her face and hands looked as if she washed them every day! My sisters have so many tangles in their hair that they look like the manes of wild ponies, but Mary's hair is always neatly tied back. But there are six children in my family and Mary has no brothers or sisters, so I decided that it was easy for her mam to keep her clean and tidy.

But it wasn't just the being clean that made her different. She seemed to be so cheerful and I thought that was very strange because her tada was dead. Jacob Jones the weaver had died when she was little. In our village, everyone knows that if there's no man in the home to bring in the money life is very, very hard. Neighbours will try to help but we're all poor. People have little enough for themselves and there's rarely much left over for others. Mary and her mam were on their own, trying to do the weaving as well as all the women's work. By the time I began to notice Mary she was already learning to thread and work the loom with her mam. The two of them were hard at it all day long; her mam on the loom and Mary cleaning, cooking, looking after the hens and bees. Work, work, work. Mam would shake her head and say, "How does the poor woman manage?"

Of course, all we children have our jobs to do. As soon as we're old enough we start to help our families. My first jobs were collecting firewood and then digging the vegetable patch and fetching the water to the cottage for Mam. Now Gwenna and little Luc often help with those things and I have other jobs. I sometimes work with Tada and my older brother Huw, out with the sheep. I like being with the men and the dogs but I don't like those other jobs. The water bucket is heavy and slops all down my leg when I hurry. Digging is the most boring thing in the world! I do my jobs as fast as I can and then I run off quick to the river in case Mam thinks of something else I can do. If she catches me I moan and make a big fuss, but when Tada calls me I go willingly.

Even though she and her mam were so poor and had to work so hard I never heard Mary grumble, even when she had to do a really messy, boring job like picking the twigs and muck out of the fleeces before they were washed. I would run past her cottage, on my way to join the other boys at the river or the ruined castle, and I would see her. She'd be sitting on her doorstep with a stinky fleece in her lap, humming away to herself. She could hardly ever go out and play like the rest of us but she would call "Good day!" as I passed her door. Sometimes she'd stop for a while, on her way to do an errand, and she'd join in the game we were playing. But then she'd say "Must be going now," and off she'd hurry.

The first time I remember speaking to Mary properly was one day when we met by the river. I remember because it was also the day I began to understand why she and her mam were different. I'd been fishing with some of the boys and my line had got tangled in a bush on the riverbank. The others had got tired of waiting and gone off home, leaving me pulling and muttering. I got it free at last and then I slipped on a wet rock and cut my big toe. Mary came along the track from the big village and there I was, limping home and leaving red dots of blood in the dust behind me.

"Good day to you, Bryn Parry," said she. "What have you done to your foot?"

"It's just a cut," I said, trying to limp faster, as if it was nothing to bother about.

"I have something that will help," she said.

"Don't trouble yourself!" I was wishing she would go away because I was feeling very foolish.

She shrugged and walked past me down the track and then she turned round.

"If you keep walking as slow as that you'll miss your supper, though you may be in time for breakfast tomorrow!" She was grinning at me, as if it was a big joke.

"Humph!"

"It must be very sore."

Well, she was right about that! My toe had started to throb as if someone was hitting it with a hammer. So I stopped and she put down her basket. First she made me put my foot back in the river and wash the blood and dust off. Then she took out the cleanest handkerchief I'd ever seen and dried my foot. After that she reached into her basket, took out a jar and stuck a finger into it. Then she spread some sticky stuff on to the cut.

"Yowch!" I yelled. She laughed at me, sitting there holding my foot and making faces.

"You'll live, Bryn Parry. Stop making a fuss; that's good honey I put on your cut. Our bees worked hard to make it."

"Honey?" I was amazed because honey is a rare treat in our family. My mam has enough to do without keeping bees as well, though there are people in the village who do. "We put honey on our bread, not on our feet!"

"Well, it will keep your cut clean and help it to heal fast," she replied, as she quickly tied the handkerchief round my foot and knotted it neatly. "There, now we can be home before supper."

We walked back to the village together and I realised that already my toe wasn't throbbing as badly.

"What have you done to yourself this time?" asked Mam when I got home. As I explained, she gasped and a look of horror came over her face.

"What were you thinking of, letting that girl put things on your foot? Wash it off! Wash it off quickly!"

"Aw Mam, it's only honey and it made my toe feel better!"

"Honey indeed! Listen to me my boy; you wash it off this very minute!"

Mam pushed me on to a stool, pulled off the handkerchief and threw it on the fire. Then she looked hard at my toe, tutting and frowning.

"What's the matter?" Ceris, my big sister was standing in the doorway.

"Watch the baby while I deal with your stupid brother!" Mam ordered her as she dragged me outside and poured a jug of water over my foot. I hopped about, shouting, "Stop, Mam! It's only honey! Where's the harm in that?"

Then Mam stopped and looked at me sternly.

"You must be careful of that girl and her family. They and their friends are not like the rest of us. They've changed. They've left the old ways that have suited us and our fathers and our fathers' fathers before them."

"But... " I didn't understand what she was saying but she wouldn't let me speak.

"They've started to follow strange new teachings that Outsiders have brought to the valley. They don't go to the church with the rest of us now. They go off and meet with others of their kind; creeping about in the dark and getting up to no good! They're no better than Mad Bethan!" She filled the water jug again and handed it to me.

"You scrub that foot and clean off every scrap of that potion. Goodness knows what bad magic she's put into you!"

More Lifepath Adventures!

In the Shadow of Idris
Ruth Kirtley

Bryn can't make up his mind about Mary Jones. She doesn't go to church any more, and his mam says that Mary and her mum have started to follow the teachings of Outsiders. But to Bryn she seems normal and kind. What will Bryn do, though, when he finds out she's about to set out on a very dangerous road?

£4.99   978 184427 374 4

A Land of Broken Vows
Steve Dixon

It's 1141, and murder and death are sweeping over England. knights, barons and kings make and break promises in order to get power and money. At the monastry of St Mary in the Wilds, John, the son of a knight, seems shut away from all the broken promises, but soon even the monks can't resist the temptation to break their vows to God. John is plunged into a world of danger and lies – will he be able to protect his friend?

£4.99   978 184427 371 3

Hard Rock
Fay Sampson

Collan can't wait to join his dad and brother as a Hard Rock man – a miner – but it doesn't take long for him to realise that the mine is a dangerous place. How will he cope having to work with his father's drunk workmate? And what difference will the visit of John Wesley make?

£4.99   978 184427 372 0

Want more action and adventure? Try these great books!

Look out for *The Lost Book Trilogy* by Kathy Lee!

The Book of Secrets

Jamie and Rob live a simple life on the island of Insh More. But Rob dreams of more, and these dreams lead both of them into mortal danger. Will the book in the seal-skin bag help them?

£4.99   978 184427 342 3

The Book of Good and Evil

For Jamie, Rob and Ali, the magnificent island city of Embra holds different paths. Jamie struggles to make a living and is constantly drawn to the book in the seal-skin bag. How will the words inside help him to cope with war, robbery and the treachery of Sir Kenneth?

£4.99   978 184427 368 3

The Book of Life

A blind beggar brings a mysterious message to the King of Lothian. An old friend needs your help... This is the start of a dangerous mission, taking Rob and Jamie far from Embra to a land of darkness, slavery and death. Will they ever be able to escape?

£4.99   978 184427 369 0

A Captive in Rome

Kathy Lee

"Where's Father?"

Conan, my brother, looked up the hill, where our dead and dying soldiers lay like fallen leaves... hundreds of them, too many to count. Faintly in the distance I heard the sound of a Roman trumpet.

A disastrous battle tears Brin's world apart. Captured and taken into slavery, he is forced to start a new life in the incredible city of Rome!

£4.99   978 184427 088 0

The Dangerous Road

Eleanor Watkins

Gwilym and his dog Brown are on their first trip taking his father's sheep to market. They'd be having a good time if Huw, the old shepherd, didn't always want to spoil their fun. But soon the dangers of the drovers' roads threaten to put a stop to their fun, and their lives altogether.

£4.99   978 184427 302 7

The Scarlet Cord

Hannah MacFarlane

Joshua is leading the Israelites towards the great city of Jericho. The army is getting ready to make its move. But on the plains in front of Jericho, four children are heading towards the greatest danger they have ever faced.

£4.99   978 184427 370 6

Fire by Night

Hannah MacFarlane

Moses is leading the Israelites out of Egypt, but for two members of the tribe of Asher, things have gone badly wrong.

£4.99   978 184427 323 2

Great books from Scripture Union

Fiction

Mista Rymz, Ruth Kirtley £3.99, 978 184427 163 4
Flexible Kid, Kay Kinnear £4.99, 978 184427 165 8
The Dangerous Road, Eleanor Watkins £4.99, 978 184427 302 7
Where Dolphins Race with Rainbows, Jean Cullop £4.99, 978 184427 383 5
A Captive in Rome, Kathy Lee £4.99, 978 184427 088 0
Fire By Night, Hannah MacFarlane £4.99, 978 184427 323 2
The Scarlet Cord, Hannah MacFarlane £4.99, 978 184427 370 6

The Lost Book Trilogy

The Book of Secrets, Kathy Lee £4.99, 978 184427 342 3
The Book of Good and Evil, Kathy Lee £4.99, 978 184427 368 3
The Book of Life, Kathy Lee £4.99, 978 184427 369 0

Fiction by Patricia St John

Rainbow Garden £4.99, 978 184427 300 3
Star of Light £4.99, 978 184427 296 9
The Mystery of Pheasant Cottage £4.99, 978 184427 296 9
The Tanglewoods' Secret £4.99, 978 184427 301 0
Treasures of the Snow £5.99, 978 184427 298 3
Where the River Begins £4.99, 978 184427 299 0

Bible and Prayer

The 10 Must Know Stories, Heather Butler £3.99, 978 184427 326 3
10 Rulz, Andy Bianchi £4.99, 978 184427 053 8
Parabulz, Andy Bianchi £4.99, 978 184427 227 3
Massive Prayer Adventure, Sarah Mayers £4.99, 978 184427 211 2

God and you!

No Girls Allowed, Darren Hill and Alex Taylor £4.99, 978 184427 209 9
Friends Forever, Mary Taylor £4.99, 978 184427 210 5

Puzzle books

Bible Codecrackers: Moses, Valerie Hornsby £3.99, 978 184427 181 8
Bible Codecrackers: Jesus, Gillian Ellis £3.99, 978 184427 207 5
Bible Codecrackers: Peter & Paul, Gillian Ellis £3.99, 978 184427 208 2

Available from your local Christian bookshop or from
Scripture Union Mail Order, PO Box 5148, Milton Keynes MLO, MK2 2YX
Tel: 0845 07 06 006 Website: www.scriptureunion.org.uk/shop
All prices correct at time of going to print.